6.00

New Girl

Published in Canada by Fitzhenry & Whiteside,
195 Allstate Parkway, Markham, Ontario L3R 4T8

Published in the United States by Fitzhenry & Whiteside
121 Harvard Avenue, Suite 2, Allston, Massachusetts 02134

www.fitzhenry.ca   godwit@fitzhenry.ca.

National Library of Canada Cataloguing in Publication
Scott, Mary Ann, 1936-
New girl / by Mary Ann Scott.

ISBN 1-55041-725-8 (bound).--ISBN 1-55041-727-4 (pbk.)
I. Title.
PS8587.C6316N48 2003   jC813'.54   C2002-905302-1
PZ7

U.S. Cataloging-in-Publication Data
(Library of Congress Standards)
Scott, Mary Ann.
New girl / by Mary Ann Scott ; cover illustration by Julia Bell.-- 1st ed.
[186] p. : cm.
Summary: Young teenage girl moves from the country to a big city and struggles with adjusting to a new school, making new friends in an ethnic community, and a new living situation with her grandmother.

ISBN 1-55041-725-8
ISBN 1-55041-727-4 (pbk.)

1. Teenage girls – Fiction — Juvenile literature. 2. Adjustment (Psychology) in adolescence – Fiction – Juvenile literature. (1. Teenage girls — Fiction. 2. Grandmothers – Fiction.) I. Title.
[Fic] 21   PZ7S4251N53 2003

Fitzhenry & Whiteside acknowledges with thanks the Canada Council for the Arts, the Government of Canada through the Book Publishing Industry Development Program (BPIDP), and the Ontario Arts Council for their support for our publishing program.

Design by Wycliffe Smith Design Inc.
Cover Art by Julia Bell

Printed in Canada

New Girl

By Mary Ann Scott

Fitzhenry & Whiteside

CHAPTER 1

I t was a great dream. Suze and I were charging down the hall of my old school, flipping waves and grins to everyone in sight. Suze and I together, like we always were. Then the alarm went off and the real world came up and whomped me.

I wasn't even in my own house anymore. I wasn't even in my own town. And I was light-years away from Suze.

I raised my head from the pillow. The clattering coming up from the kitchen would be Gran. Mom never gets up until the last possible moment, but Dad's heavy footsteps were clomping around on the floor above me, then clomping down the stairs. They paused outside my door.

He rattled the doorknob. "Don't go back to sleep, Kat," he said. "Are you decent? Can I come in?"

I rolled my eyes and grunted a yes. The door creaked open. Dad is a big man with a big voice, and this morning it was ultra cheerful, revoltingly cheerful.

"First day at your new school!" he said.

"Great," I said. "Small-town girl hits big-city school and goes splat." I heard the panic in my voice, one-hundred-percent genuine panic.

"Aw, Kat," he said. "Give it up, will you? We're here. Accept it."

I sat up. "I accept it," I said.

"A little enthusiasm would be nice."

I flung myself back onto the bed. "I'm wildly enthusiastic," I said. "I can hardly wait. New school! Wow!"

He stared at me with these big, hurt eyes. This is the man who spent the first twelve years of my life pestering me to share my thoughts. About everything — TV programs, brands of cereal, last year's teacher versus this year's teacher, whatever. Until I hit grade eight, when I told him, quite nicely, that there were certain subjects I'd rather talk about to my friends. That was when I developed an "attitude" and a "smart tongue."

Recently, my "attitude" had become "negative" — meaning it was Dad who wanted to move here, and me who didn't. Up until moving day, the only place in my entire life that I had ever lived was in Heron Lake, Ontario. The town, which has the same name as the lake, is sort of hilly, with water on two sides, an absolutely perfect beach, one grocery store, one post office, one bank (where Dad worked), one medical clinic, and a general store with video racks in the back. There are two schools: the public school where I went from kindergarten to grade eight, and the high school I got yanked out of before I was even halfway through grade ten. There were three hundred and seventy-three students in that school and I knew almost every one of them by name, even the country kids who came in by bus.

My new school had over a thousand students, a thousand total strangers. Sophisticated, big-city strangers.

I swung my legs over the side of the bed. "I have to get up now," I said. "Big day."

He smiled. I smiled. Then I pulled a sweatshirt on over my nightgown and tore up the stairs to the third floor.

The last time we'd visited Gran the attic was just a storage space full of dusty boxes and moldy trunks. Now it was a bed-sitting room for Mom and Dad, with built-in cupboards where the roof slants down, and huge new windows across the front and the back. They even have their own washroom.

Mom was still in bed, snoozing. I was in and out of the shower in three minutes flat. Then I borrowed her robe, wrapped a towel around my hair, and slid in beside her.

I nuzzled my head into her shoulder. It was soft, like the rest of her. Everybody says I'm her spitting image. We have the same dark-brown, wavy hair, the same hazel eyes, and sort of the same face, I guess. Mom's heavier than I am, though, and she's got more curves, like about ten times more. I keep telling myself that I'm just a late bloomer and that super curves will happen, any day now. I've been telling myself that for the last three years.

She groaned. "Panic attack," she said. She and Dad were starting school today, too, at some hot-shot computer place downtown.

"You're having a panic attack? You're an adult, and you'll have Dad right beside you the whole time. I'm only a kid, one kid all alone."

Her lips curled up at the ends. "My panic attack is much worse than your panic attack."

I stifled a smile. Dad's always complaining about how Mom and I whine at each other. As usual, he just doesn't get the picture. It's a game: competitive whining. I'm more tired than you are. You have better clothes than I do.

Mom stretched, then reached over and squeezed my hand. "Today's a day for being brave," she said.

I made a blowing out, yeah-sure kind of sound.

"You know what?" she said. "A couple of weeks and we'll feel like we've been here forever."

"No way! Heron Lake is forever. Suze is forever. And Tyler."

"Well...," she said. "They'll always be important. But with the bank closing, we couldn't stay there. You know that."

It was the same old argument, the same sick old argument, and I still didn't buy it. Sure, the bank was closing, but that didn't mean we had to leave. We'd talked about the things we could do, all last year.

Then, all of a sudden, there was this supposedly fantastic computer school Dad just had to go to, and then Mom decided she was going too. And then it was all Toronto, all the time, and nothing I said made any difference.

"After today, I'll never see you," I said. "You'll be so busy with all your computer stuff, you won't have time for me."

She snorted, and bolted out of bed. "Pardon me for living!" she said. "But aren't you the same person who was complaining, quite recently, about being treated like a two-year-old?" She grabbed Dad's robe, slipped her arms through the armholes and knotted the belt tight around her waist. "And now you're saying we won't have time for you?"

"That was different," I said. "That was before. Who am I going to talk to here?"

"You'll be fine," she said. She nodded toward the two new computers set up on the two new computer desks. "We'll be right over there, every evening. And there's always Zoe."

Zoe is my grandmother, Dad's mother. "I can't talk to her about...stuff."

"Stuff?" Mom said. "Since when did you talk to me about stuff? If you had..."

I winced. "You didn't tell Gran about that...uh, party thing, did you?"

Mom's mouth flattened. "Your father told her," she said.

I grabbed Dad's pillow and drilled it across the room. "I can't believe he told her that!" I wailed. "The most embarrassing thing that's ever happened to me, and he blabbed it! To my grandmother, of all people! What's he trying to do, humiliate me?"

Mom reached out her arm toward me, like she was going to give me a hug, but I stopped her dead. "I'm not in the mood," I said.

Gran has carpet on her stairs, so nobody heard me coming until I was almost in the kitchen. Then they stopped talking, mid-sentence. I hate it when they do that.

Dad was washing apples, Mom making sand-wiches. "Zoe will take you to school, Kat," she said. "We won't have time."

"She doesn't need to do that. I can go by myself."

Mom glared at me. I scrunched up my face and mouthed the word "no."

Gran whipped into the room. She's almost as tall as Dad, but she's skinny. "This isn't Heron Lake," she said. "It's downtown Toronto. You'll find it extremely different from what you're used to. Extremely."

"I appreciate the offer, Gran," I said. "But it really isn't necessary."

She ignored me. That's another thing I hate, being ignored. "Eat your breakfast," she said. "The sooner we get there, the better."

I already knew what was for breakfast. Porridge.
It stunk up the whole house. "Isn't there any cereal?
Like Raisin Bran or…"

Gran's eyes met mine. "Packaged cereal is vita-
min-fortified cardboard," she said.

Dad winked at me from behind Gran's shoulder,
but Mom wouldn't look at me. The message was
loud and clear: nobody was coming to my rescue.
I'd get porridge or nothing. And there was no way I
was going to school alone. My grumpy old grandmother would be with me the whole way.

CHAPTER 2

The only time I ever changed schools was when I went from grade eight to grade nine, which doesn't really count because my whole class came too. We met at the old school and walked up the hill together.

Setting off down Gran's street that morning, I had absolutely no idea what I was getting into. In the back of my mind was this little fantasy that it might not be as bad as I thought. I was wrong; it was worse.

I didn't know what it would be like, getting lost inside a very large building — a building with five additions, one of them an addition on an addition.

I had no idea how it would feel to arrive at a classroom door (already shut, because getting lost had made me late), explain myself to the teacher, then stumble to my seat while the whole class checked me out, head to toe, with several stops in between.

And I didn't have a clue that less than a third of the kids at my new school would be white. Not a clue. It just never crossed my mind. I'm not prejudiced or anything, but it was an extremely weird feeling, like I'd just landed in a foreign country.

I was a disaster when Gran and I walked up the steps into that school; by lunchtime I was a blithering catastrophe. I took one look at the huge, crowded cafeteria, stuffed my lunch bag back into my backpack and went home. To Gran's.

It's only a ten-minute walk, but I nearly died from the cold. The air was damp and clammy, and after a few minutes it started seeping down my neck and up my sleeves. There was a dirty wind, too, and the snow was filthy, covered with little specks of soot.

By the time I got to Gran's and rang the doorbell, I was in a stinker of a mood. I hated the climate and I hated the school, and I wasn't having terrifically pleasant thoughts about my parents either. Standing there waiting for Gran to let me in was not a high point of my life. And she was taking her own sweet time coming. I sort of jabbed at the bell button in case it hadn't worked the first time, and when she still didn't come, I leaned on it. When she finally opened the door, she had a towel around her head and she didn't look all that thrilled to see me.

"You took your lunch!" she said. "I didn't expect..."

I brushed past her into the tiny vestibule, past the coat hooks and the rubber mat where we're supposed to leave our boots.

"I thought I lived here," I said. "I wasn't aware I had to have advance permission to get in the door."

"Kat!" she said. "What's—"

I didn't answer. I was already halfway up the stairs. I didn't even take off my coat. I was wearing runners, not boots, but I didn't take them off either. I just threw myself on the bed and buried my head in my pillow, my own pillow, the one I'd brought from home. It still had my at-home pillowcase on it.

Half an hour later I gulped down my sandwich, washed my face, cleaned my teeth and tiptoed back downstairs. Gran was nowhere to be seen, but there was a piece of paper with my name on it on the hall table. Lying on the paper was a key. Under the key was a little heart she'd drawn. It was the heart that got to me.

I stuck my head around the kitchen door. She wasn't there, but the basement light was on.

"Gran?" I said.

She came to the bottom of the stairs.

"I'm sorry."

"We all have bad days," she said.

When I arrived home later that afternoon, I was so polite I hardly recognized myself. I left my coat and runners where they belonged, washed up, and went out to the kitchen to help make dinner. My job, Monday to Friday.

Gran has wrinkles, but she's not what you'd call grandmotherly. Her hair is gray, shoulder-length and fuzzy with natural curl. Mostly she wears jeans and sweatshirts. Because she's so tall and skinny, they look really good on her. She doesn't act like your typical grandmother, either. She's not the least bit lovey-dovey. My personal opinion was that she was kind of sour. Dad said that wasn't true; she was just uncomfortable showing her feelings. But I think he's kidding himself. Even though I'm her only grandchild, I'd never been totally sure she even liked me. I could have been wrong about that though. That little heart thing was nice.

The other thing about Gran is that she has to know absolutely everything that's going on, like it's her right to be told stuff. Seriously personal stuff. When I turned thirteen, she asked me if I had my periods yet, and last year she wanted to know if any of my friends were having sexual relations (her words, not mine). I mean, I didn't even know. I sure wasn't, and I'm ninety-nine percent sure Suze wasn't — but even if we were, I'd hardly be blabbing to Gran about it.

She handed me a vegetable peeler and nodded toward the counter at a paper bag of potatoes and a pile of big thick carrots. Then she started in on me.

"So, how was it?" she said.

I shrugged. "Crowded." I started peeling my potato into the sink. It was a different kind of peeler than I was used to. A queen of peelers. Slick.

"Watch that thing," she said. "It's addicted to human flesh." She was chopping away at some onions, then dumping them in a huge black pot. "What about the teachers?" she said. "Did they seem helpful?"

I shrugged again. "I guess," I said.

"And the work? Are you ahead, or behind, or...?"

I sighed. "I don't know yet, Gran."

"You were there for a whole day," she said. "You should have some feeling about where you stand."

I really didn't know about everything yet, because I'd only had some of my classes. But if I didn't answer her, I'd end up feeling stupid. I handed her my first peeled potato. "I don't get the feeling I'm ahead," I said, "but it's kind of hard to tell."

She rinsed my potato under the tap and plopped it into a bowl of water. "Keeps it from discoloring," she said. "I take it you don't enjoy school that much."

"I don't know anybody who actually enjoys it." I picked up another potato. So far I'd only skinned my finger once. A tiny nip, nothing serious.

"Perhaps you've heard this before," she said, "but what you get out of school depends on what you put into it. And on the kind of friends you choose." She looked at me sideways, checking to see if I got the point.

I had heard it before, and I did get the point. Mom and Dad blamed Suze for everything: my attendance record, my marks, the trouble we got into last summer, everything. It never seemed to occur to them that Suze had exactly the same problems, and that her mom blamed me.

"Did you meet anyone yet? Talk to anyone?" Gran said.

"Not really. Nothing, you know, meaningful."

She turned the heat on under the pot, poured some oil in, then stirred the onions around with a long wooden spoon. "It must be...unsettling," she said. "A new school, a new environment, no friends..."

Sympathy can be deadly, especially when you'd rather die than cry. I rinsed off my second potato and picked up my third. My eyelashes were a little damp and my throat ached something fierce, but I didn't break down.

When dinner was in the oven, I went upstairs, to my room. Mom and Dad's old computer was set up on my desk, all ready to go. I clicked on e-mail.

Dear Suze,
School here sucks. Except for the teachers, not one person spoke to me or even smiled at me the whole day. I mean, is that pitiful or what?

I miss you so much! And I'm frantic about Tyler. I just know he's going to fall madly in love with that new girl in our house who's supposed to be so stunning-looking and brilliant and everything and you'll probably be best friends with her and I'll just be forgotten, like I'm dead or something, like I never even existed.

I blew my nose, read what I'd written, then deleted it. I sounded like a sick sheep.

Dear Suze,
My new school is huge! There are so many people it's like some mob scene you'd see on TV! Hardly anybody in the whole place is white, which knocked my socks off at first, but when you think about it—that people here come from all over the world—it's awesome.

Saying good-bye to everybody was absolutely devastating, so the minute I got in the car I started weeping, and of course Dad couldn't just leave me alone and let me get over it, he had to start picking at me. Again. Like, I totally overreact to everything, I think nobody but me ever had to change schools, I have no sense of adventure, and I've never challenged myself, whatever that means. Then Mom got on Dad's case because he was on mine and it was like one of those TV programs where everybody's sniping at everybody else, only this was real life, and it went on and on, until I finally got the bright idea of pretending I was asleep.

I haven't made friends with anybody yet, but the kids here are extremely cool and REALLY into style. Everything's kind of exciting and scary at the same time, if you know

Chapter Two

what I mean.

What's the new girl in our house like? Is she nice? Is she as pretty as everybody said? Gran redecorated my room. She even sponge-painted the walls. AND she made me a new bedspread AND curtains, both out of this really sweet mauve-and-blue flowered stuff with white lacy ruffles. It's like something out of one of those decorating magazines your mom gets.

Write to me. I miss you so much! I can still see you there standing in the driveway, all bundled up in your mom's fur coat, waving and waving, getting smaller and smaller, until you were gone. Or we were, I guess.

Your forever friend,
Kaitlin Zoe Avery

CHAPTER 3

On my second day I learned how to move through a crowd without getting any of my tender bits crunched. What you do is hold something hard, like a binder or a backpack, so it covers your boobs and your nose, and just barrel through. And you keep close to the walls. The problem is you look like a total idiot when you're doing it.

This weird girl in math class showed me that. She'd been waiting at the front of the room, just standing there at the door, until everybody left but me.

I know perfectly well you're not supposed to judge people on how they look, but the math-class girl is definitely not my type. Suze is my type. She's probably the best-dressed person in the whole school, and she's totally laid back. The math-class girl's clothes were topped by a man's ripped jacket that came almost to her knees, and she was so intense she bounced. But what really turned me off was her greasy blonde hair. I mean, style is individual. But hygiene, that's basic.

Her voice was fast and loud and super cheerful, sort of like Dad's in the morning. "Hi!" she said.

"I was wondering, like, what you're doin' for lunch? Seeing as how we're both new, and the cafeteria is, like, way scary..."

I'd seen the cafeteria, of course. It's in the basement of one of the additions and it's so big it has pillars holding up the ceiling. The way you get there is from these open stairs that twist down from the main floor, so you get a view of the whole place before you're actually in it. What you see is hundreds of little round tables crammed together around the pillars. Every single table has four or five people sitting at it and a few more lurking around, waiting to pounce when somebody gives up a chair. Standing there, looking down at all those people chattering and yelling and sharing homework was the loneliest feeling in the world.

"So...lunch?" she said. She was so bright and eager she was pathetic. There was no way I was going into that place with this person.

"I go home," I said.

"Oh." Her eyes flicked away from me. When they flicked back, she was grinning. "I'll walk you to your locker then," she said.

I just looked at her. I couldn't think of a way to say no without sounding rude.

When we came to the stairs, I paused. "My locker's up there," I said.

"Sure," she said, like her locker was up there too.

The whole upstairs floor had already emptied

out, which made it easier to walk. And talk, unfortunately. She asked me where I came from, and then I sort of felt like I should ask her the same thing, so I did.

"Oh!" She waved a hand. "I'm from here, from Toronto. I dropped out for a while, then, when I decided to drop back in, it seemed like a good idea to change schools. To get away from certain people."

"So, you moved, or what?" I said.

"I moved, but I'm gonna have to move again. You don't know anybody who has an extra room, do you?"

I shook my head. "I don't know anybody, period."

Her face turned pink. "I just thought...I mean, I'd sort of like to get in with a family."

"We live with my gran, in this tiny little house..."

"You and...?"

"My mom, my dad, my gran, and me."

My locker was half the size of the ones in Heron Lake. I pulled my jacket out, shrugged myself into it, and stuffed my backpack in its place. Then I gave her a little wave, and turned to leave. She came with me.

"You're Kaitlin, right?" she said.

"Kat. Kat Avery."

"I'm Erin. Erin Orme."

She was zipping along beside me, her head turned toward mine, telling me what a great school this was, or something. A great school academically, that's what she said. Lots of scholarship winners.

I was sort of listening and sort of not listening, partly because I wasn't all that interested in what she was saying, and partly because we were getting close to the top of the stairs. Too close. One more step and she'd be a goner.

I plucked at her arm. "Watch out!" I said.

She collapsed against me and hung on like her life depended on it. "I can't believe I almost did that!" she said. "If you hadn't stopped me..."

I pried her nail-bitten, cuticle-shredded hand off my arm. Then all the way down the stairs, all the way to the main door, she kept bleating on about how I'd saved her life, and how that made her obligated to me, like forever. "I could have broken my neck!" she said. "So I owe you. Big time. Until I save your life back."

"You're not obligated," I said. "Anybody would have stopped you!"

"You're just embarrassed," she said.

I was, and I had the hot cheeks to prove it. I gave her one of my don't-push-me looks, zipped up the neck of my jacket and shoved my shoulder against the outside door.

"I won't forget," she said.

"Whatever," I said, and ran down the steps. That's when things got really weird. I could feel her eyes following me all the way down the street, and she wasn't even standing there watching me—I checked. It was a bizarre feeling, like her eyeballs were bouncing along behind me, attached to my back with string. Sort of paranormal or something. I don't even believe in stuff like that.

Gran had made tomato soup, my very favorite cold-weather lunch. Gran crumbles her crackers on top. I float mine, then sink them with the bottom of my spoon. Square crackers, with butter.

"Nice technique," she said.

"Mom thinks it's gross."

Gran shrugged. "How was this morning?"

It was my turn to shrug. My turn to ask a question. "If you save somebody's life," I said. "Is that person... obligated to you? Until they save your life back?"

She shook her head and made a little "tsk" sound with her mouth. "That's just superstition," she said. "Who saved whose life?"

"It's not important."

Her spoon hung in the air, and her eyes held mine.

"It was just this girl," I said.

"Um-hmm."

I took a delicious, squishy mouthful: soup, soggy crackers, butter. Yum.

"Did someone really save her life?"

"No! She could have fallen down a couple of stairs, that's all. Somebody yelled at her and she pulled herself back." I lowered my eyes to the bowl and scooped some more soup.

Gran cleared her throat. "Were you the one who yelled at her?"

My jaw felt so tight it ached. "It was nothing, Gran," I said. "Nothing. Believe me."

She did something with her eyes then, sort of a Dad thing, like some miserable kid had just hurt her feelings. On purpose. That's when I gave up. She was good at this interrogation stuff, really good.

"She wasn't paying attention to where she was going," I said, "so she could talk to me better, I guess. It was dumb. We were practically at the stairs. They're really steep there, too."

Gran was smiling. "It sounds to me like she's fairly enthusiastic about getting to know you. Which is rather nice, isn't it?"

I winced. "It wasn't anything meaningful, Gran."

She leaned back against the bench. "Well, if you've made a friend, that seems fairly meaningful to me."

I buttered two more crackers, then floated them. "She's not a friend," I said.

Gran took another spoonful of soup and suspended it in front of her, almost at her mouth, but not quite. "What's wrong with her, then?"

"She's just not my type."

I'd had enough—enough soup, enough crackers, enough questions. I shoved my bowl away and slid down the bench.

Gran's eyes shifted to the clock on the stove,

then back to me. "This is interesting," she said. "In what way is she not your type?"

I sighed. "She's just weird, that's all."

"Weird in what way?"

"She isn't...cool. I only met her about an hour ago, but she was following me around the school, almost like she was stalking me. She even wanted me to have lunch with her, just because we're both new."

"Maybe she's lonely too," Gran said.

"It's more than that, Gran. She was trying too hard, and her clothes are...I don't know, too weird."

Gran's eyes narrowed. She folded her arms and leaned toward me. "She's not dark-skinned, is she? If this is prejudice on your part, I'll be extremely disappointed in you. Extremely."

I stared at her, hard, but I didn't go ballistic or anything, which was some sort of miracle because I was totally insulted. "I'm not like that," I said.

Gran reached across the table to touch my arm. "Sorry."

For some peculiar reason I really wanted her to understand. "It's hard to know what kind of a person she is," I said. "She seems...rough. She dropped out of school for a while, too, and, I don't know, I get the impression she's living on her own. The whole thing's just too strange. She's not like Suze at all."

Gran nodded. "And Suze is the perfect friend?"

"Yup," I said.

The next day, I met a guy. His legs were stretched across the aisle, blocking my way to my seat, which was just behind his. When I tapped his foot with the toe of my shoe, he moved.

His elbow hung casually over the back of his chair and when he smiled, his eyelids dropped so he was looking at me through these little slits. I didn't smile back. Suze and I have this thing about not making total idiots of ourselves around exceptionally cute guys. Then I messed up. I blushed. Then I got embarrassed about blushing, so I blushed even more.

"I'm Pavel," he said. He passed his glance up and down my body. My face flamed.

I already knew his name. It was only my third day in that school but this guy was the hottest topic in the girls' washroom. I knew what movie star he was supposedly identical to. I could point to three of his ex-girlfriends and two of his current favorites. And when I took the last stall near the window, I could read the sign-up list of eleven wannabe favorites, their measurements, and what parts of their bodies were pierced. Half the female population of the school sucked up to him. It was, "Hey Pavel, you wanna see my tattoo?" and, "Hey Pavel, you think I'm thin?" and, "Hey Pavel, you like thongs?" Sick-making stuff. And they were always touching him. There's no way I'd behave like that. Not ever, not for anybody, movie-star clone or not.

Dear Suze,

You won't believe this, but the absolute cutest guy in the whole world sits right in front of me in English!! He's sort of Tyler-looking only more so, half Tyler and half that lifeguard from the beach last summer, the blond one, only this guy (his name is Pavel) is dark—dark hair, dark eyes, and eyelashes to die for.

I also met this loser girl—Erin—who is really short, doesn't live at home, and is totally uncool. She was actually following me around the school, wanting to be my friend!!! Now I have to figure out how to dump her before people start thinking she's my best buddy or something.

Mom and Dad spend all their time in the attic, working on their computers, which is where our TV is.

I can't even use the headphones, it would be a "distraction"! Gran has a TV, too, only she watches these really boring public affairs programs, so I'm stranded.

Write to me. I'm dying!

Love, Kat

CHAPTER 4

I learned the floorplan of the school. I learned the
teachers' names and what they expected of me. I
said "hi" to at least four people in every class. I
smiled so much I got a sore face. But I still didn't
know anybody.

Every day I missed Suze, every minute. I missed
the notes we passed in class; I missed the little
nudges we gave each other in the halls; I missed the
silly jokes we told, the kind that are so stupid they're
funny. But after school, I missed her the most. That
was when we'd hang out, listening to CDs, trying on
each other's clothes and, when they weren't around,
our mothers' clothes. And their makeup. Suze was
the sister I'd always wanted, the perfect sister: the
one you can say anything to and she'll understand,
the one you know as well as you know yourself.

I missed Tyler too. There was this special place we
used to go, down by the lake. The pine trees were
thick there, but in the middle, there was this little
grove carpeted in needles. We had our first kiss
there, our first sweet, shy kiss. We went back there a
lot after that. Until Dad found out, and started lurking

around the dock, messing with the boat. Spying on us.

Missing Suze and missing Tyler were totally different. Other than a page full of kisses and hugs, I hadn't written to Tyler at all, because I couldn't think of anything to say. I could write a book to Suze, I could write a book every day. I only wished she'd write back.

The only people I knew in my new school were Pavel and Erin. I saw Pavel a couple of times in the hall, but he never saw me. I never saw Erin. Not that I wanted to see her. I wanted to see her *first*, so I could get away. In my worst nightmare, I'd tear around the corner by my locker and there she'd be, parked, ready to go into her heavy friendship act.

But I didn't even catch a glimpse of her, not once; not until she breezed into the next math class. After class, just like before, she waited.

"You brought lunch?" she said.

"I told you. I go home."

"Never mind," she said. "I'll walk you to your locker again. I've got this amazing idea. You'll love it, I know you will."

I groaned as we headed up the stairs, an inside-the-head groan. I hate it when people tell me I'm going to love something. I feel pressured, and when I feel pressured, I get confused. If I don't love whatever it is, I have to wonder if I really and truly don't love it, or if I'm just being pig-stubborn.

Erin looked at me sideways. "You want to meet people, don't you?"

I nodded. I did. People I wanted to meet, though, not people who got foisted on me.

"If you promise to bring your lunch," she said, "absolutely promise, I'll get us a table in the cafeteria. Tuesday. After math again. And I'll bring somebody else too, so it won't just be me."

I stood there at my locker, staring at her, trying to keep my jaw from dropping. Not only did she know I wasn't all that stuck on her, she was actually telling me she knew!

I made a quick recovery. "You're skipping math to get a table?" I said. Suze would have done that; she cut classes all the time. She always had a note though. She could fake her mom's signature perfectly.

"I don't skip," Erin said.

"Then how can you be sure you'll get a table?"

"It's no big deal. You just have to get there early."

"Why are you doing this?" I said. "Like, why me?"

She looked away from me, into the distance. "It's tough making friends," she said. "Especially when you come in the middle of the year, when everybody's already tight with everybody else. And you're not exactly..."

Clean, I finished her sentence in my head. Then I felt like an absolute worm. Lower than a worm, an amoeba.

"Anyhow," she said. "You'll come?"

"Sure."

"You will?"

I wanted to bite my tongue off. She hadn't expected me to come! She thought I'd say no!

I fumed about that for hours. I wouldn't go, I
couldn't go. Going meant kissing my social life
good-bye for years! When you hang out with a
weirdo, people think you're one too, and then no
one would be caught dead being your friend. Except
the weirdo, of course.

Suze would have understood that perfectly. I even
knew what she'd say. First, she'd dump all over me
for agreeing to go in the first place, then she'd come
up with a plan. "Just tell her right out you've
changed your mind," she'd say. "Or, if you're too
chicken for that, get sick. Stay home that day. Who's
to know?"

Erin would know, that's who. And I would know.
That was the part Suze might not understand.

It had been snowing all afternoon, big fat flakes of it.
Everything looked so clean it reminded me of Heron
Lake, only the houses are bigger there, and so are the
yards. In Gran's part of Toronto, everybody lives so
close together you can't walk between your place and
your neighbor's with your arms stretched out. Actually,
you can only walk along one side of Gran's house.
The other side is attached to the place next door.

We've got this little pimple of a front porch and a really tiny fenced-in yard, so there's hardly any sidewalk and shoveling (another of my little chores) took only a minute. There's an alley running behind the houses where the garages are and everybody has a path between the alley and their back door. That's what I shoveled next. Then I checked out the garage. The plow had been by but it left a lot of icy, crusty stuff behind so the garage doors were frozen shut.

I was chopping away back there, lifting and swiveling, when I heard scraping sounds from next door. I poked my head around to see who it was.

There was a guy there, and he was pitching snow like he was mad at the world. We saw each other at exactly the same time. I recognized him immediately; he wasn't quite so sure of me.

"Don't I know you from someplace?" he said.

"I'm Kat," I said. "English class. I sit behind you. You're Pavel, right?" As if I didn't know.

He nodded, like he'd figured out who I was all by himself. "You live here now? The old lady moved out? She was a right bi—"

"My gran," I said quickly. "She didn't move out. We moved in."

He smiled his slow, lazy smile just for me, like it would wipe out what he almost said. "No offense," he said. "She, uh, called the cops on me. When the parents were away. Didn't like my party, I guess." His eyes focused somewhere behind me for a moment.

Then he moved a couple of steps closer and leaned his folded arms on his shovel. "They're going away again soon," he said. "Florida. Maybe we can make a deal. You interested?"

I shrugged. "I don't know. You have to tell me what it is."

He was smiling and nodding his head at the same time. "I invite you to my party," he said. "And you get the old lady to back off with the cops. Then we'll both win, right?"

I had to laugh. The idea of Gran agreeing to a scheme like that was hilarious. "She won't go for it," I said. "No way."

"She'd call the cops on her own granddaughter? She might say she would, but…"

I hacked at some ice with the edge of the shovel. "It must have been some party."

"It kind of snowballed. You know how it is."

My mind flashed back to a moonlit beach and a pile of trouble. "Yeah," I said. "You invite, like, twelve people, and you get fifty."

"Exactly." He swept his hair out of his eyes and frowned. "How come you don't wanna come to my party? Girls always wanna come to my parties. You don't like me or what?"

"I want to," I said. "But…"

A door slammed behind him. Pavel turned. "Hey Cuz," he yelled. "Come meet the new girl. See if you can change her mind."

This guy was taller and thinner. He peered into my face. I peered back into his. He looked kind of dazed.

"This here's Alexei," Pavel said. "My cousin. He needs a girlfriend real bad, eh boy?"

I blushed, but neither of them noticed. One second they were standing in front of me; the next, Pavel was flat on his back, screaming blue murder, trying to keep Alexei from stuffing snow down his pants.

Gran was rolling pastry when I came back inside. Her friend Marion was sitting at the table, drinking tea. She and Gran are almost direct opposites. Marion is plump, top-heavy, and short. She used to walk with a cane, but now she needs a walker. The last time I'd seen her, which was probably last summer, her hair had been in a long white braid. Now it was red, cropped close to her head, and curly.

The great thing about Marion is how she's always glad to see me. She's actually kind of gushy, something I usually hate; but Marion's a sincere gusher, not a fake one. So when she launched into "how you've grown" and "I'm so glad you're here, dear," I knew she meant it.

"I see you've met that young troublemaker from next door," Gran said.

"Which one?"

"Pavel." She spewed out his name like it left a bad taste in her mouth. "We're having quiche. Wash your hands and you can grate the cheese."

"I thought maybe you meant Alexei," I said. "He was giving Pavel a snow bath, washing his, uh..."

Then I started breaking up, because all the words I could think of for that particular body part were not words I wanted to say at that precise moment.

Marion and Gran were watching me, waiting to hear what part of Pavel was getting washed, I guess; probably thinking it was his face or his neck or something. I was trying not to laugh, and of course that made me break up even more.

But Marion was laughing, too, so maybe she'd guessed. "Washing his...?" she said.

"His thing!" I said. "Alexei was washing Pavel's thing with snow! I mean, he wasn't actually washing it, he was dumping snow down his pants, but Pavel was screaming at the top of his lungs, like he was getting killed or something, only he was screaming in a different language and Alexei was screaming right back and..."

"Well now," Gran said. "That will cool that conceited little so-and-so off. He's charming, of course, when he wants to be, but..."

"But?" I helped myself to a nibble of cheese.

Gran's eyes flicked sideways. "I suppose you think he's handsome?"

"Pavel? Sure. I mean, he is! Those dark eyes and... Yeah, he's handsome all right, but he's got groupies, Gran. I don't go for guys with groupies. There's too much competition."

That's when Marion told me how willowy I was getting, and how attractive, and how competition wasn't something I had to worry about. (Nobody in my whole life has ever said I was pretty. It's always been "attractive," which I guess is better than being unattractive, but still...)

Gran took a glass pie plate from the cupboard and measured it against the rolled-out pastry. "Groupies," she said. "That sounds like a sexually transmitted disease."

"Gran! Groupies are fans! A group of fans. They're all over him. I mean they're really all over him. It's pretty disgusting, actually."

"I wasn't aware you knew him," she said. She folded the pastry in half, lowered it onto the pie plate, then unfolded it again and pressed it into place. "So you wouldn't go out with him?"

"He'd never ask me," I said. Then I laughed. "Well, actually, he sort of did."

"No!" she said. She'd been running a knife along the outside of the pie plate, trimming the crust into a circle, but now she stopped dead. It's probably hard to trim a pie crust when you're busy looking horrified.

"He did!" I said. "You wouldn't believe what he wanted me to do!"

She laughed a sharp, bitter laugh. "I wouldn't put anything past that one."

"I'm supposed to convince you not to call the police when he has his next party. Because supposedly,

I'll be at it."

She dipped her fingers in a cup of water and pinched the edges of the crust. "And what did you say to that?" she said.

I was grinning so hard I could hardly get the words out. "I told him you wouldn't go for it."

Marion laughed. Gran nodded, then she smiled. She looked almost happy. For a moment, anyway.

We stood together at the kitchen window, looking out. It was dark, and the outside lights were on: the one behind the house and the streetlights in the alley. There was no sign of Alexei, but Pavel was still shoveling. I wondered how it was we hadn't bumped into each other before, on the way to and from school. Different schedules, maybe. What the groupies wouldn't give to live right next door to Pavel!

"He was a beautiful child," she said. "Full of life. I used to make cookies for him." Her voice was sad, like she'd lost something important. "Now he gives me the finger."

So much for Pavel, then—I had my loyalties. But after supper, I looked "willowy" up in the dictionary. Then I danced around in my room, flipping my hair and darting glances at myself in the mirror. Lithe, slender and graceful? *Moi?*

CHAPTER 5

In a perverted sort of way, you had to admire Erin, the way she went for what she wanted. After school, there she was, just outside the main door of the school, lying in wait.

"I thought I'd walk with you for a bit," she said.

For a change, she wasn't right in my face, all eye contact and everything. She looked at the mob of people pouring out of the school behind me; she looked at the bare trees across the street; she looked at the filthy crusts of snow along the road; she didn't look at me.

I couldn't figure out what was going on. Then, when she finally did look at me, there was something different in her eyes. I almost got the feeling she was saying "please" under her breath.

"So, I can walk with you?" she said.

"Sure." I fanned my face with my hand: the second-hand smoke was fierce. The smokers light up the minute they get off school property.

Erin fell in beside me, and we crossed the street. Everybody did, all at once, so cars coming from both directions had to stop dead, right in the middle of the block. If they hadn't, they would have run us down.

"You really want to get to know people, right?" she said.

"Of course I want to know people!" I said. "Not just anybody, though."

I was trying to be honest, to let her know I wanted to make my own friends. But being honest and being tactful at the same time isn't all that easy. Anyway, if I did bruise her feelings, she got over it pretty fast. Her voice was as spunky as ever.

"Being passive doesn't work, you know," she said. "If you want something, you have to get right out there and fight for it."

I had to laugh. "Is that why you're following me around? I already said I'd go to lunch. You don't have to hassle me about it." I was sort of ticked off, but sort of flattered at the same time. Only I wasn't about to let on about the flattered bit.

"You're pretty prickly," she said. "But that's okay. I'm prickly, too, sometimes. We'll get along just fine."

The way she was going on, it was like we were going to be best buddies for the next twenty years. "I don't know about prickly," I said, "but you sure are pushy."

"I'm just being friendly! You want me to leave, just say so!"

I didn't say anything. I didn't want to encourage her, but I couldn't be mean either.

When we stopped at a traffic light, she laughed. "You're right, though," she said. "I am pushy. But I'm smart, too. You don't know that yet, but I am. Uh, how are you getting along in math?"

That was a low blow. I wasn't doing all that well, and Erin knew it. The teacher had had a little talk with me. He wasn't sarcastic or anything, he just said I had some catching up to do. "It's not my greatest subject," I said.

"Did you get question four?"

Question four was a killer; I'd already spent almost an hour on it. "It's not due until tomorrow," I said.

"If you want, I can show you how to do it."

It was a bribe. If I'd take her home with me, she'd help me with my math. "I'll be okay," I said. "My dad's good at stuff like that."

We passed four houses in an uncomfortable silence. I broke it first. "How's it going with the move?" I asked.

She sighed. "It's really hard to find a place. Where I am now, I don't have anywhere to leave my stuff." She jerked her head toward her backpack. "I have to carry everything I own around with me, or leave it in my locker. Otherwise I get ripped off."

I was shocked. "That's not very good," I said.

We were almost at Gran's. I figured I'd just walk right by, then, when we got to the corner, I'd peel off, head down the lane, and deke in the back door.

Only I couldn't do it. I stopped in front of the

house. "This is where I live," I said. "I have to help my gran, now. With dinner. It's this agreement we have. I do it every day, or I don't get my allowance. I mean, it's not all that much, but..."

"I don't have time, anyway," she said. "I'm going to the library, to do my homework. The people there are really nice, really helpful."

Maybe she was trying to tell me something. Really nice people, really helpful. Unlike me.

Dad isn't above a little bribery, either. When he and Mom finally decided we were moving to Toronto, he promised me my own e-mail address, on my own computer. "That way you can talk to Suze whenever you want," he said. "It'll be great. Almost as good as a phone call."

Only it wasn't working out like that. I'd been waiting to hear back from her for days. Then, when the message finally came, it wasn't just from her; it was from Tyler, too. He doesn't have e-mail, so they were at Suze's place, but at two-ten in the afternoon, where they should have been was in English. And Suze's mom worked, so they were alone.

The first and last bits were from Suze. Tyler's part was in the middle.

Dear Kat,

I miss you like crazy. Nothing is the same
anymore. Everything is boring—home,
school, life, everything.

The new girl, Penelope, is pretty boring, too.
(She's a seriously serious person. Seriously.)
Yesterday I made the mistake of calling her
"Pen" and she had a snit-fit, which I guess you
can get away with if you're drop-dead beautiful, but I was NOT impressed. I mean, she
could of just asked me not to call her that. I
mean, if I knew it got up her nose so much, I
wouldn't have done it. Anyway, the guys here
are falling all over their feet trying to get her
attention, and the girls, except for me, are
seriously peeved. I could care less.

My idiot mother has a new boyfriend,
Sleazy Arthur, the guy who ran the canteen
at the beach last summer. Three times now
he's offered me money to get lost, so he and
Mom can be alone. I mean, am I totally
grossed out or what?

Love,
Suze

Hey Kit Kat!
He shoots, he scores! I got two goals against
the Dragons last week, but we lost anyway.
The ref was thick, blind, and biased. Suze
came to the game. She hitched a ride with
George Kaftin, who was wasted. She's been
hitching a lot, which is seriously stupid,
right? Maybe you can talk to her. She won't
listen to a word I say.

Be good,
Ty

Dear Kat,
Tyler is turning into a SNITCH! I got turfed
out of the house on Saturday. What was I
supposed to do, freeze to death in a snowbank?
S.

I must have read that message ten times. Maybe
I was adding two and two together and getting five,
but it was easy to be suspicious. At the beach party
last summer, the one I got in such hot doo-doo
about, a lot of kids—couples—left the campfire and
went off into the woods. Suze went with Kenny
Ricken, who has probably the worst reputation of
any guy in the whole school. After Suze and Kenny

left, and then some other people left, Tyler asked me if I wanted to go too. He didn't do a number on me or anything, he just asked. There was no way I was going, but I knew he really wanted me to.

Like I said, it was easy to be suspicious.

I was like a dog chewing a bone, working on that math question. I even went back over the chapter, and then I went back over the chapter before that. I always thought that the questions were supposed to illustrate the points in the text, but with this one, I couldn't see any connection. Finally, I figured out something and took a stab at it. I knew it wasn't right, though. That's when I bundled everything together and took it upstairs.

Dad didn't have a clue. Math has changed a lot since he went to school. Mom didn't have a clue either. "Why don't you ask Zoe?" she said. "She's the teacher in the family. She only retired a couple of years ago."

I'd totally forgotten that. She'd even taught math, and to grade twelves!

It took her about three minutes to figure out where my problem was. "How many classes did you miss last term?" she said.

"A couple. Three, uh, maybe four."

"Sick, were you?" She has really beady eyes. I'd never noticed that before.

"Not always."

She dropped her head to the table. When she brought it up again she sighed, then started flipping back through the book. "Let me guess," she said, "you missed this chapter, and...probably this one, too."

I flipped through the same chapters. I'd never seen them before in my life.

Her eyes were boring into mine. "Those chapters are integral to the whole course. You know what integral means?"

I felt like an idiot. "Necessary?"

She nodded, a stern school-teacherly nod. "What surprises me is that you're doing as well as you are. The answer you worked out is wrong, but I must say, it's fairly ingenious. Well, where do we go from here? Shall we retrieve those lost chapters?"

I dropped my head to the table. I still had history to read, and some questions to do on that. Then there was my science assignment, and...

It was one-thirty when we finished. She helped me with everything, but except for the math, when she was leaning over my shoulder the whole time, she was just around and about, in case I needed her. The cool thing was she actually seemed to be having fun. Mom and Dad always groan when I ask for help, like they begrudge me the time. They don't say so, they say I should learn to be self-sufficient, but I get the message.

I was totally beat, but there was one thing I had to do before I crashed.

Dear Suze,
Thanks for the letter. I guess it kind of surprised me, though, you and Tyler writing it together. Was that supposed to be some kind of a message? Are you going out with him or what? If you are, I can handle it, I just need to know.

The movie-star clone (who lives next door!) asked me to a party, but I probably won't be able to go. He's a wild man, and Gran knows, so I'm cooked.

Love,
Kat

P.S. Tyler is right. Hitching is a seriously stupid, no-brainer thing to do. I couldn't STAND it if anything happened to you. So stop!

Chapter 6

It was Tuesday, lunch-with-Erin day, and I knew exactly how it would be. She wouldn't get a table and she'd feel really bad about it and I'd end up feeling sorry for her. Or the other girl wouldn't come, and ditto. Or the other girl would come, and I wouldn't like her either; only then I'd be stuck with the two of them. Forever, probably.

But first, there was math. We worked through the assignment, the so-called killer question; marked each other's papers, then handed them in. My little heart was going pit-a-pat the whole time, but it wasn't from terror. It was from pride. I got it right.

Erin sat in the front row; I was near the back. The deal was she'd zip down to the cafeteria ahead of me, and I'd follow.

Finking out was still an option. Maybe I could have done it if I hated her, but I didn't hate her. I even sort of liked her sometimes. I just didn't want her for my best friend.

The cafeteria was swarming with people. I was clinging to the railing, trying to keep from being swept down the stairs, when I saw her. She was

standing beside the only empty table in the place.
When she saw me, she started waving like a maniac.

She screamed my name out at the top of her
voice. "Kat! Kat! Over here! Over here!"

I made a stiff little wave in return, then, cringing
with embarrassment, maneuvred my way across the
room. She was wearing the same clothes she always
wore, and her hair was stiff, like she hadn't rinsed
all the shampoo out.

"So, am I smart or what?" she said.

A huge note was taped to the top of the table.

! Please !
Save this table for four new girls
(Chairs too)

"Four girls?" I said.

"I told you there'd be more than me." She swung
her eyes toward the table beside us. "Don't look
now," she said, "but we're being watched."

Being watched didn't begin to describe what was
happening. Being on center stage was more like it.
Practically everybody was staring at us, and a lot of
them—guys—were making comments.

"Hey, new girl!" somebody said. "Where you from?"

"Who's your friend?"

"Hey, can I have one of those chairs?"

We ignored them. They got worse.

"New girls, new girls, new girls," they chanted. It was

cheerleader stuff, not full volume, but loud enough.

I covered my eyes with my hand. "I'm probably beet-red," I said.

"They'll stop soon." Erin jumped to her feet and cupped her hands around her mouth. "Danielle! Over here!"

"New girls! New girls! New girls!"

I was so embarrassed for that poor girl I could hardly bear to look, but when I finally did, I almost fell off my chair.

She was striding toward us, waving and smiling like a nominee heading into the Oscars. Only she wasn't your usual nominee type: she wasn't glitzy, and she wasn't the least bit anorexic. She was tall and sturdy, and she had one of those ultra-cool hairstyles black kids have, a whole head full of long thin braids that flipped around when she moved.

The cheerleaders whistled and hooted, but Danielle sailed right up to them, raised one finger to her lips and stood there, waiting for silence.

Her voice was soft and deep. "Hush, little ones, hush," she said.

Except for one clown who started crying like a baby, the little ones hushed. Even the clown hushed when one of his friends elbowed him off his chair.

Erin clapped and I laughed.

Danielle smiled a wide, super-white smile. "Wow!" she said. "Two people to have lunch with! Fantastic!" She turned to me. "You're Kat?"

I grinned. "How did you know what to say to those guys? If that had happened to me, I would have been, like, totally self-conscious."

"I have a brother," she said, like that explained everything.

I laughed again, which is what I do when I'm embarrassed. I was embarrassed because I couldn't stop looking at her. Her skin was like coffee with cream in it, and she had a beautiful face—not just pretty, beautiful. Enormous eyes, dark and bright at the same time; long thick eyelashes; cheekbones to die for.

Erin was standing again. "Sarita!" she yelled. "Over here! Sarita!"

Sarita grabbed her waist-length hair, twisted it into a knot, and slid gracefully into the fourth chair. She had a neat little head, tiny sharp features, and a bright, birdlike way of looking around her.

"I brought extra lunch," she said. "To share." She passed around a bag of little pastry triangles stuffed with something spicy and delicious. "It's Indian food," she said. "Because I was born in India. But we lived for two years in England and a year in Capetown and another year in Vancouver before coming here. And you? Where are you from?"

"Quebec," Danielle said. "La belle province. I miss it. And school is so hard here! But my dad got transferred, and—"

"Quebec schools are easy?" I said.

"No! It's the language thing. The English."

"You don't sound French," Sarita said. "You don't have an accent."

"My dad is English, and I always had English friends, so speaking is okay. Even reading isn't all that bad. It's writing that kills me. I'm going to have to work my butt off this year."

I told them about Heron Lake. "It's not even really a town, it's that small," I said. "But it's beautiful. I miss it a lot. I knew everybody in my whole school."

"You sound sad," Danielle said.

I shrugged. What could I say? I was.

"Well, I'm from California," Erin said. "But we lived in Mexico for a while, too. That was before we came to Canada. Then my dad died. He was a pilot, and there was a problem with the plane. It was up north somewhere. I was just a little kid, so I don't remember. After that, my mom, she married again and moved back to California."

"She's there, and you're here?" Sarita said.

"She didn't want it to be that way," Erin said. "But her boyfriend didn't want me, and... The thing is, she's gorgeous, my mom. Men would kill for her. Rich guys. And she's kind of weak that way. She likes the big bucks."

"So she dumped you?" Sarita said. "For money?"

Erin shrugged. "She put me in a foster home," she said. "She figured I'd be better off. Her boyfriend is a bit of a loose cannon. You never know what he'll do next. I mean, he could be in jail by now, for all I know. She dumped Jimmy, too. He's my brother. I haven't seen him since I was seven."

I frowned. Danielle and Sarita were frowning, too.

"That's rough," Danielle said.

I nodded. "Really rough. But you could look for him, couldn't you? At least that would be something, to have a brother."

Sarita brushed her foot against mine, a signal I wasn't sure how to read.

"I don't know his last name," Erin said. "We had different fathers. So, you want to do this again? We could have lunch together every day, if you like."

Every day? I snuck a glance at Danielle, then at Sarita. Sarita raised her eyebrows. "I can't commit to something like that. My work load is obscene."

"Mine, too," I said quickly. "I'm behind in stuff. Seriously behind, like in math. Maybe once a week?"

"Once a week would be perfect," Danielle said.

Sarita nodded.

Erin crunched her lunch bag, then drove it into the nearest garbage bin. "I can't believe you guys," she said. "What a bunch of wimps! I work four hours a day, every day, and I missed a year of school, so I'm taking an extra course. I have time for lunch, though. I mean, we have to eat, and talk to people, and..."

Danielle shrugged. "The only time I can go to the library is at lunch," she said. "What about Saturday? Not every Saturday, but... We could meet at one of those coffee places on Queen Street."

"Saturday?" Erin said. "If I'm lucky, I'll be working. If not, I'll be out pounding on doors looking for work. Maybe you can spend the weekend sitting on your bum drinking coffee, but I sure can't. If I don't work, I don't eat. It's called survival. You guys haven't a clue about how poor people live. Like, I have friends who have to go all over the city just to get fed. They get a free meal in some church down the street one day, but if they want to eat the next day too, the only place they can go is right across town. And they have to walk, because they haven't got the money for streetcar tickets. And then they wear out their shoes. And you can't even wash your feet except in public washrooms, which is also how you wash everything else, even your hair. With hand soap. From a dispenser, if there is any. And dry it with paper towels."

I avoided looking deliberately at Sarita and Danielle. This was too weird.

"Well," Danielle said. "Let's set something up by phone, at a time you can make it. We can at least do that."

Erin laughed, but it was a bitter laugh. She peered into the empty pocket of her jacket. "Oh darn," she said. "I seem to have mislaid my shiny new cell phone."

Danielle pulled a pad of sticky notes from an outside pocket of her backpack, then scribbled her phone number three times on as many bits of paper. "Call me from a pay phone," she said. "Borrow a phone. Just do it, Erin. Or give me your work number and I'll call you." Then she passed around the notes so we could put down our numbers too.

In spite of Erin's little lecture on poverty, I felt good about lunch. Good enough to push myself a little and try to make a friend on my own. My next class was history. I bounced in and looked around.

Lanni, who sat behind me, was the obvious choice. I liked the look of her; she kind of reminded me of Suze.

The teacher was late for class, so I swiveled around in my seat. "Hi," I said.

She looked up from her books and flicked her eyes over me, checking me out, for my fashion statement, probably, which was fine with me. I didn't have the upscale labels she had, but I looked okay.

"Hi," she said. Her voice sounded bored. She turned a page and studied it closely.

I'd been going to ask her something about her haircut, like where she got it done or something but her attitude was putting me off. What actually came out of my mouth sounded kind of pathetic, even to me.

"I'm new," I said.

She didn't take her eyes off the page. "Oh, yeah," she said.

Depending on your tone of voice, "oh, yeah" can mean just about anything. It can mean "tell me more" or "that's cool" or "seriously?" or even something incredibly rude, like, "I should care?" From the flat way Lanni said it, and the way she didn't even bother to look at me, her message was clear. My being new—my being there—meant zip to her, absolutely zip.

I didn't say anything after that. There wasn't much point. I just turned around again, feeling empty, like all my breath had been sucked out.

Lanni wasn't one bit like Suze. Suze would never be rude like that. Never!

Marion was just moving her walker into the front room when I got home. Gran was coming down the hall behind her, carrying a tray. On it were a teapot, two mugs, and a plate of chocolate-chip cookies that were still warm from the oven. I held my hand over the plate and raised my eyebrows.

"Take your coat off, wash your hands, then come and join us," she said.

"Yes, ma'am," I said. I turned on my heel and goose-stepped into the kitchen.

"So," Gran said, when I returned, "how was lunch with Erin?"

"Lunch was okay," I said.

"You're still not sold on her?"

"She's still weird," I said. "But I liked the other two girls."

Gran's left eyebrow rose. "Nice girls, were they?

Friendly? Not, ah...weird?"

I snaffled another cookie. "I like them fine," I said.

"Bring them home," Gran said. "Bring Erin, too. She interests me. I'd like to meet her."

I thought about that later. Sarita and Danielle were great, but they were all tied up with Erin. Making friends with them, and not with her, would be extremely difficult.

CHAPTER 7

It had been a major storm. Two days later, only the main streets had been plowed. Lots of people were flipped out about that, but we got at least as much snow in Heron Lake, and we coped just fine.

I was drifting along the road on my way home from school, daydreaming, pretending I was back there. The lake would still be covered with snow. You could see it from the top floor of the school, and from the Pine Street hill on the way home, and when you turned into our street, it was right there, in our backyard. I could picture every house on that street, name every family—name every kid, actually.

I looked around at the houses on Gran's street, wondering if I'd ever get to know the people here. Probably not, I thought. Probably you have to live in a small town for that to happen.

There was a guy ahead of me on the road who was poking along even slower than I was. When I cruised by him, he broke into a wide smile.

"You are next-door girl!" he said. "I am Alexei."

"Pavel's cousin!" I said. "I thought you were just visiting. You live there?"

He nodded. "Since three months. Since I came from my country." He named a place I'd never even heard of, couldn't even pronounce. "It is a very small place," he said. "With a very big war."

"Moving is hard," I said.

"It is very hard." His eyes slid away from me. "A new country, a new home..." Then he looked at me again, and grinned. "I study English very much. You wish to help me? You would be a very nice teacher, a very pretty teacher."

I laughed. "Your English is okay."

"Speaking is okay," he said. "Not perfect, but okay. Reading and writing are most difficult. You will come to my house? We will have a nice time, yes?"

"Uh..."

"You do not wish this? It is trouble for you?"

I smiled. "I'd really like to come," I said, which was true. There was only one small problem. "It's just that my gran and Pavel have this feud thing going. I'm not sure..."

"Ah, Pavel! Pavel is small boy with small brain." Alexei's mouth was serious but his eyes were laughing. "You come," he said. "Come today. I will make tea for you. Auntie Irena will be home." He gave a solemn little nod. "Auntie Irena is very correct. No messing around with girls when Auntie Irena is there."

I laughed. "Sure, I'll come," I said. "Why not?"

It was weird being in that house because it was the other half of ours, and they were mirror images of each other. Their front room was to the right of the door, not the left. The stairs were opposite, too. The kitchen was in the same place, in the back, but the appliances were all switched around.

We sat in the dining room. Auntie Irena stayed in the kitchen, but she kept an eye on us. I soon got the feeling it was just as well she did.

"Pretty girl," Alexei said. He made an hourglass shape with his hands, which was my first clue that this guy's mind was seriously deranged. My breasts are the size of half oranges. Small oranges. Mandarins.

He patted my hands a lot, then lifted my hair up to admire my neck. "In my country, girls are very sexy," he said. "You are very sexy girl, also. You know this?"

The blush started at my neck and moved down and up at the same time. Did this guy have only one topic of conversation?

"I embarrass you," he said. "I will stop. You wish to see my schoolbooks?" He brought his backpack in from the hall, then upended it on the table. "You have these books also? We can do our homework together."

Pavel was wrong about him. It wasn't just a girlfriend he wanted, he wanted a tutor too. I sorted through his books. The only one we had in common was math.

I flipped through it, to the killer question. "Have you done this one yet?" I said.

He shook his head. "It is too difficult. I must complete it for tomorrow, but..."

I tore a page from his binder, then went through all the steps Gran had gone through with me, explaining as I went.

He thought I was brilliant. He kept picking up my hands and kissing them, and the whole time he was doing it he was staring at me through these thick, straight eyelashes. Kissing a woman's hand is the European way, he said. He knew, because he'd been to Italy on his way to Canada. He could even speak a few words of Italian. *Amore* was one of them. That means love. He said some other words too, but he wouldn't tell me what they meant.

"You are perfect," he said. "Pretty, smart, kind..."

He was older than the guys I knew and he had all the right words, and he made me feel older too. But also sort of lighthearted and giddy at the same time, like I was dancing through the trees in a beautiful pine forest, wearing a swishy black dress and oodles of eye makeup, and high, high heels. Showing off my lithe, slender, graceful body. And underneath all that, temporarily hidden, was my brilliant, mathematical mind.

The whole experience was a gas, but it was getting late; I had to get out of there. Gran would be starting to stew about where I was, and why I wasn't home yet. The last thing I needed was her mad at me.

I'd made apple crumble for dessert, and the empty dish was sitting in the center of the table, the crusty bits still stuck to the rim.

"There's this guy," I said. "Alexei. He lives next door. He asked me to help him with his homework. At his place."

Gran snorted. "Cousin of the wretched Pavel."

Dad poured cream into his coffee, then added four spoonfuls of sugar. "Pavel?" he said. "Wasn't he the little kid who used to toddle over here for cookies?"

"That little kid," Gran said, "has grown into a conceited, rude young man, with absolutely no respect for his elders. Who, according to his own mother, runs through girlfriends like a lawn mower through dandelions."

Mom frowned. "Just how well do you know these boys, Kat?"

"Pavel's in one of my classes. He's fine, he's nice."

Gran's eyes fastened on mine.

"He's fine with me," I said. "Alexei's different. I met him on the way home from school today, and he invited me in for tea. You'll like him. He's not like Pavel at all."

"You went in that house?" Gran said. "With that boy?"

I sighed. "Auntie Irena was there. He told me

she was, before I went in. I'm not an idiot!"

She scooped the dessert bowls into a pile, and disappeared into the kitchen. Mom followed her as far as the doorway.

"What if Alexei comes over here, Zoe?" she said. "How do you feel about that?"

Gran's voice was sharp and high. "Up to you," she said. "She's your daughter. I'll tell you one thing, though. There'll be no hanky-panky in this house!"

I flopped my head forward. "Give me a break," I said.

After supper, I checked my e-mail—for the fifth time that day. It had been four days since I'd sent that message to Suze, the one about her and Tyler, and I hadn't heard back. Which could only mean one thing. She was feeling so guilty about what she'd done, she couldn't even tell me.

The two of them probably couldn't wait for me to leave. I could just see them—the whispered promises, the secret kisses. I guess I'm not half as smart as I thought I was, because when we were leaving, when Suze was standing by the car, saying good-bye to me, she had her arm around Tyler. I figured she was just comforting him, or maybe leaning on him because she needed comfort. I guess I had the wrong sort of comfort in mind.

Having a broken heart sounds romantic, but it isn't. It's horrible, and it hurts. There's this heavy feeling where your heart is and even if it goes away for a while, like when you're asleep, as soon as you wake up and remember what happened, it comes back and whomps you.

CHAPTER 8

Noon is the worst time for crowds, and I was fighting them all the way, going up the stairs when most of the school was coming down. Danielle, on the down side, tapped me on the arm as she passed and stepped smartly from her stream into mine.

She squeezed her eyes almost shut. "Tell me you're going to the cafeteria!" she said. "Please say yes! Please!"

"I haven't anything to eat, and I haven't any money either. I usually go home."

She hit her forehead with her hand. I knew how she felt; facing the cafeteria on your own is scary. Then I thought of the alternative, of bringing her home with me. That was scary, too.

I'd never once, in my whole life, brought anybody home that I hadn't known, like, forever. And our Heron Lake house was beautiful. White, with dark-green shutters and a steep roof, it nestled on the side of a hill, looking over the lake. It was nice on the inside, too, with crisp white curtains and light pine floors and soft, pretty colors.

Gran's house, except for my room and the third floor, is old and crowded and gloomy. But even if Danielle lived in a really rich place, which she probably didn't, she was much too nice to be a snob.

I invited her quickly, before I lost my nerve. "You could come home with me," I said. "It's only a ten-minute walk. I mean, the house is kind of old, but..."

"It'll be okay with your parents?"

"They won't be there. My gran will. She told me to invite you." I looked around the hall. "You and Erin and Sarita."

"She really said that?"

"Yes! She'll be delirious. She'll ask you a thousand questions. You probably won't even have time to eat, but..."

"I have to call home," she said.

Outside, she slipped her backpack to the ground and pulled a cell phone from an inside pocket. I don't understand French all that well, but what happened next was a typical parent-kid conversation in any language. The kid explains the problem, then listens while the parent lays down the law. Then she rolls her eyes at her friend, and puts her hand over the receiver. "My mother wants to talk to you," she said. "Sorry."

What her mother wanted was my name, my address, my phone number and a complete list of who'd be home when we got there. She was quite nice about it all, but still...

"Don't mind her," Danielle said. "She's never lived outside Quebec before. We have to check in every time we move."

"Is that Sarita?" I said. "Let's—"

Danielle shot her arm out, holding me back. "Erin will have a cow," she said.

I'd seen glimpses of Danielle in the hall before, and I'd seen Sarita too, and I was pretty sure they'd seen me, but we'd never made contact. I'd thought it was because they weren't interested. Now I wondered if Erin had been weighing them down too. I felt a rush of annoyance. She didn't own us.

"It's not like we're deliberately excluding her. If we see her, we'll..."

"Never mind," Danielle said. "It isn't Sarita, anyway. It's somebody else."

Gran just loved Danielle; she asked her zillions of questions, and Danielle answered them all. Most of them were about Erin.

"I'm curious about her," Gran said. "She doesn't live with her family?"

"I don't think so," Danielle said. "She says things like, 'I need a new place'. Never 'we need one'. So you just assume she's alone."

Lunch was canned baked beans on toast, with ketchup. Danielle divided her egg sandwich three ways, and Gran put out a plate of sweet pickles, and later, some cookies.

"She had a boyfriend," Danielle said. "Last year. But he split. That's when she left home, I think. I'm not sure, though. Another time she said it was her foster mom who had the boyfriend."

Gran frowned. "Aren't her parents in the picture?"

Danielle turned her palms toward the ceiling with a shrug. "The other day, she said her mother was in California and her father was dead, but before that, she told me her mother was dead and she never knew her father, so..."

This was news to me. "How come you're so interested in her, Gran?" I said. "You've never even met her."

Gran shrugged. "A young girl alone... Maybe she needs help."

"I think she might have even been a street kid," I said.

Danielle nodded in agreement. "Maybe she still is one."

"You should check that out with her," Gran said. "If she's in a bad situation, there may be things we can do to help her out."

"I don't know," Danielle said. "Sometimes she really resents it if you ask her stuff. Other times, it's like she resents it if you don't. She's kind of a mystery, actually."

The traffic light near the school is rigged against pedestrians. We get about fifteen seconds to cross the street, and if we miss the light, we wait about five minutes for another chance.

A streetcar clattered past, dinging its bell. Horns tooted and the beat of amplified music blared from passing cars. Pedestrians, bundled against the cold, scurried along the sidewalk. Behind us, a group of frozen looking preteens huddled in the doorway of a video arcade.

"Your gran is super," Danielle said.

"I guess," I said. "She's been tutoring me in math and I'm actually starting to like it. Is that scary, or what?"

"Look!" she said. "Over there, by that red car, in front of the library. It's her—it's Erin. She's talking to a guy."

We crossed the street, trying not to stare. The guy was wearing one of those really soft-looking leather jackets and he was making choppy motions with his hands, like he was really mad about something.

"Keep walking," I said. "She'll never even see us."

Danielle shook her head. "Maybe she's in trouble. Maybe she needs help. We have to ask."

"We do?"

"Uh huh. It looks like he's doing a real number on her. What if he's trying to get her to buy drugs or something?"

When we came up behind them, Erin was raking

her hands through her hair. "You promised you'd
stop hassling me!" she said. "You promised!"

The guy, who had to be at least as old as Dad,
was so ticked off he was practically spitting his
words out from between his teeth. "I just want you
to try it," he said. "That's all I'm saying. Just try it."

Danielle tapped Erin on the shoulder. "Are you
okay?" she said.

Erin's eyes slid from Danielle to me, then back
to Danielle. "I'm just freaking wonderful," she said,
and stomped off down the sidewalk.

The guy unlocked the driver's door of the red
car, then just stood there, watching Erin leave.

Danielle raised her eyebrows. "Another mystery,"
she said. "I wonder who he is?"

"Boyfriend?" I said.

Danielle shrugged. "Too old. I'd sure like to
know what he wanted her to do."

"Something she hates," I said.

Five minutes later, before I even had my coat off,
Erin was ripping down the hall toward my locker.
"That was fast," she said.

"What was fast?"

Her eyes were hard. "Don't play your innocent
little games with me," she said. "The dump-Erin
thing you just did. You and Danielle."

I rolled my eyes to the ceiling. "She came home

with me for lunch," I said. "It wasn't planned, Erin. It just happened."

"Was Sarita there?"

"No!"

I hate fights. I hate them so much I'll do anything to stop them—even something incredibly stupid, like inviting someone I hardly even like home for lunch. "You can come another time," I said.

She grinned her little-kid grin. "Great," she said. "When?"

"I'll have to ask Gran."

A couple of minutes later, I had another visitor. Pavel had been sauntering down the hall when he snapped his fingers, caught me by the arm and backed me into the wall.

"Saturday night!" he said. "The big party. You talked to the old lady yet?"

People were looking at us. There were girls out there who would commit murder to be in my position. Even Lanni, six lockers away, was watching.

"I talked to her," I said. "She wasn't exactly overwhelmed."

"Come anyway," he said. "No way she'll call the cops if you're there."

I shrugged. I'd never get to that party. Never. "I could be busy," I said.

He squeezed my arm just a little too hard, then took off again. "Just come!" he called. "You'll have fun. Everybody has fun at my parties."

I slid my eyes toward Lanni. She waved at me. I didn't wave back.

The letter on the hall table was ultra thin, thin enough to be an empty envelope, someone's idea of a joke; but it was from Suze, and she isn't a joker.

I ripped it open. It was more a note than a letter, a note like you'd pass in class: a few words on a ripped-off corner of lined paper.

> You nit, it's not me he's going out with, it's Penelope!
> S.
>
> P.S. Don't e-mail me, our computer has a virus.

I squeezed my eyes shut, slid my back down the wall and crouched there, clutching my gut. Gran, who'd been standing in the kitchen, wiping her hands on her apron, moved in on me. "Bad news?" she said.

I shook my head. "Stupid," I said. "I did a dumb-dumb."

"That bad?" she said. She squatted down beside me.

I handed her the note. "I thought Tyler was going out with Suze," I said. "But it's Penelope."

"Penelope?"

"The new girl. In our old house."

Gran nodded a few times, then she read the note. "Which is worse?" she said. "Tyler and Suze, or Tyler and Penelope?"

"Tyler and Suze would be worse. Much worse."

"You'd feel you lost them both," she said. "And this way it's only Tyler?"

I nodded.

"Half the pain," she said.

Jealousy is horrible. It makes you hate people you don't even know. I'd never met Penelope; I'd never even seen her. But every time I thought about her, I hated her a little bit more. I hated her living in my house. I hated her going to my school. I hated her talking to my friends; but when I thought about what she was doing with my boyfriend, I really hated her.

I didn't hate Tyler, though. Even if I wanted to—and sometimes I did—I couldn't. I just missed him. Sometimes when I closed my eyes I could almost see his face, almost hear his voice. I had to stop doing that though. It made me cry. Then my eyes got red and my nose dripped and I looked ugly.

Anyway, you can't hate somebody just because they've been honest. Tyler told me, straight out, that when I moved it would be all over between us. It was me who said we should wait for each other. I'd go back, I said. I promised I would. I'd find a way. We'd write to each other, and some day, after I finished school and got a job, I'd go back, and he'd be waiting, and everything would be perfect, just the way we'd planned. We'd be like Mom and Dad, highschool sweethearts who grow up and get married and live happily ever after.

He didn't believe I could do it, that I could go back like that and get a job, and everything. At least, that's what I thought then. Now I'm not so sure. Maybe he didn't want to wait that long. Or maybe he wasn't all that busted up about me leaving in the first place. If he wanted a different kind of girlfriend—and I think he did—he was probably happy I moved. And I was so stunned, I never got it.

Snail Mail
Dear Suze,
I met ANOTHER really cool guy who lives next door! This isn't Pavel, the movie-star type I mentioned before, it's his cousin who lives with him. Alexei, that's his name, has only been in Canada for like, three months or something. Anyway, he's EXTREMELY nice, the funny and teasing kind of nice, and really tall and skinny. His eyes are bright blue and they disappear when he laughs and his hair is so straight it's like porcupine quills. I'm going to be helping him with his homework—in our house, unfortunately. I'm not allowed to go to

his. Gran's convinced that Pavel's evil influence will pollute me.

AND I'm having coffee this Saturday with my three new friends! Danielle is half French, from Quebec. She's, like, BIG, and amazingly beautiful, and super confident and DEFINITELY not what you'd call a flashy dresser or anything. Most of the time she wears overalls. She's got great hair, though. It's in cornrows.

Sarita is sort of like us, only a whole lot smarter. (No offense, but what can I say? She's this absolute perfectionist about homework.) She's short and dark and really into fashion and she ALWAYS wears black. And always something cool, but not skin tight or anything. She was born in India but she talks like she was born in England. Only sometimes you can tell she wasn't, like there's an accent on the accent.

Erin I already told you about. She's the weird one who's always getting her underwear in a twist. I spend half my time trying to convince her that I like her as much as the others, which is hard, because I don't.

Write to me. New friends are so NEW. Half the time I don't know what to say to them.

Love,
Kat

P.S. Thanks for the note about Tyler and Penelope. It wasn't exactly what I wanted to hear, but it's a whole lot better than what I thought.

CHAPTER 9

The coffee shop where we'd arranged to meet was on a street of small stores—dry cleaners, hair salons, ethnic restaurants. And on every corner, a mom-and-pop grocery store. The day was mild, and fruit and flowers and vegetables were displayed right out on the sidewalk.

The place was buzzing. A stack of free neighborhood newspapers sat on the ledge of the large front window. Erin grabbed one, then turned to the *Help Wanted* section.

"I thought you had a job," I said.

"Maybe there's a better one out there."

We were sitting at a table in the back, past the glassed-in counter where the cakes lived. Sarita and I sat against the wall, Erin and Danielle across from us. Sarita was stirring honey into her tea, but she was looking at Erin. "You work in a restaurant, right?" she said. "Are you a waitress, or what?"

"I'm whatever they want me to be," Erin said. She sipped her coffee, looking over the rim of her mug. "It's a small place. I do everything."

"My uncle has a restaurant," Sarita said. "You

do kitchen stuff or serving-food stuff?"

"What's the name of it?" Erin said. "Maybe I can get a job there. Anything's an improvement on the cockroach-and-mouse-infested-disgust-o-mat I work in now."

"Remind me never to eat there," I said. Danielle shivered, but Erin and Sarita ignored me.

"It's in Vancouver," said Sarita. "Did you ever find a new place to live?"

Erin shook her head. "Still looking."

Sarita divided her date square into four pieces and shared them out, all the while focusing on Erin. "Where do you live now?"

"Great date square," Erin said. "I live with a bunch of jerks, actually. They keep ripping me off."

Danielle pulled her braids behind her head and fastened them with a clip. "Your stuff gets stolen?" she said. "Like what?"

Erin shrugged and looked at her backpack. "Clothes."

"I can't believe this," Sarita said. "What kind of lowlife would do that? Why do you stay?"

Erin shrugged again. "It beats living on the street."

Danielle and I exchanged significant looks. "In Quebec, we have foster parents," Danielle said. "They must have them here, too."

Erin was beginning to look flustered. "Been there, done that," she said. "Could we talk about something else?"

I laughed. "You sound just like my friend Suze. That's what she says when I start bugging her. Like the time we were at this beach party and she went off into the woods with this guy, and I was thinking, like, the absolute worst. Then, when I asked her about it, she got all snippy on me, like I shouldn't even need to ask her something like that, like I should know better or something. And then she said, 'Can we talk about something else?'"

Danielle frowned. "So, what do you think? Did she or didn't she?"

I drained my mug. "The thing is, the guy has this really bad reputation. So I did sort of wonder."

"Is she a good friend?" Sarita said.

"Yeah, the best. Since I was in kindergarten. And we promised each other, cross-your-heart-and-hope-to-die, that we'd tell each other absolutely everything."

I thought about how I'd kept my part of the bargain. Nothing went on in my life that Suze didn't know about. Even the embarrassing stuff: like the time when Tyler and I had just started going out and he walked right into our clothesline, and my padded bra was practically dangling on his nose.

"What's so funny?" Danielle asked, so I must have been smiling.

I changed the subject. "Do you remember stuff from kindergarten?" I said.

Sarita amazed us by rhyming off the name of every kid in her class.

"I don't remember names," Erin said. "But I remember something. I slapped the teacher's face."

We all looked at her. "Why?" I said.

"She put me on the spot. She asked me to read something out loud and I couldn't do it. I thought she'd asked me just to embarrass me, and I don't know, I just flipped, I guess." She laughed heartily. "I had to sit in the time-out place and I was so totally humiliated! Anyway, I learned my lesson. I'm very nice to teachers. I've never slapped one since."

When we were outside again, Sarita and Danielle turned one way and Erin and I the other.

"I have a favor to ask," Erin said. "It's kind of pushy, but..."

I had this sinking feeling in my stomach. I didn't say anything, though; I just kept walking along beside her.

"I'm desperate for a shower," she said. "I was wondering if I could take one at your place."

"Now?" I said.

"Yeah. I'm rank."

"I'll have to ask Gran. I can't imagine her saying no, but..."

Erin shoved a cigarette package from the sidewalk onto the street with her toe. "It's taking advantage," she said. "I know it is, and I wouldn't ask if it wasn't absolutely necessary. But there's no one else. I'd rot before I asked Sarita, I get the feeling she's looking down on me all the time, from a great height. I felt like an insect under a microscope in there."

"She asks a lot of questions," I said, "but she doesn't mean anything by them. She's just interested. We haven't known anybody like you before, so we're curious. What about Danielle? Could you ask her? Another time, I mean, not now."

"She has a brother."

"You don't like guys?"

"Let's just say I don't have a whole lot of trust in the ones I've met. Especially when it involves taking my clothes off."

Gran was really nice to Erin, but she kind of blew the whistle on me.

"I'm so happy to meet you, dear," she said. "I've been telling Kat to bring you home, and now she has!"

Erin nudged me in the ribs with her elbow. I could have sunk through the floor. I could have kicked them both.

Gran's voice was all bright and cheery. She never talks like that to me, never. And she never calls me "dear," either. "Kat," she said. "Will you see that Erin has everything she needs? Towels, shampoo..."

I tried to make my voice bright and cheery, too. "Sure," I said.

Then Gran went really overboard. "Erin, if you'd like to run your clothes through the washer and dryer while you're here?"

Erin was practically flattened with gratitude; there were actually tears in her eyes. "You don't mind?" she said. "I have some other things too, in my backpack. I mean, I didn't bring them because... I have to keep them with me, or..."

"They get stolen?" Gran said.

Erin nodded.

"And Kat," Gran said. "If you'll lend Erin something to wear, then she can wash everything at the same time."

It wasn't like I had a choice. I looked at Erin. "You want to come up to my room?"

She was dying to get up to my room. I think she was sort of embarrassed though. She knew I wasn't exactly thrilled, which made me embarrassed too. I mean, being in snot mode isn't exactly gracious behavior. I was trying to hide it, trying to act like I was just fine about the whole thing, but the truth is, I was royally teed off.

While Erin was in the bathroom doing her thing, I was sitting on my bed, trying to get a grip on myself. I felt sorry for her, I really did. I couldn't imagine not being able to take a shower every day, and not having clean clothes. Then Erin stuck her head around the door. Could she use the deodorant? Could I give her some Tampax? That just fractured me. There are some things you just can't do without.

She stayed for supper. We had to eat in the dining room because the kitchen table was too small. Erin told her California story, and her dead pilot story and her rotten foster-parent story. I hadn't heard that one before, but she said it was one of many. That even if the parents were okay, the other kids living there weren't.

She looked spectacular, especially her hair. It was soft and shiny and almost-white blonde. Mom and Dad really liked her. Gran loved her. It was a dream relationship for everyone but me.

When Erin finally left, and Mom and Dad went back up to the attic, Gran invited me into the front room, for a little talk.

"I hope you aren't having uncharitable thoughts," she said.

"Did I say anything? Did I make one word of complaint?"

"No," she said. "But I wasn't a teacher for forty-some years for nothing. I have a pretty fair idea what you're thinking."

"Yeah, well, what I'm thinking is that Erin Orme has been using me. Playing this heavy friendship thing, sucking up to me. And it's not even because she likes me, it's because she needs help. But I'm not a moral idiot, Gran. I know her life is awful."

"The bottom line," Gran said, "is that she's trying to make changes, and she needs help to do it."

"I know, Gran. I know. I'm trying, I really am.

She just rubs me the wrong way."

Later, when Gran was watching television, I snuck the clothes Erin had borrowed down to the basement and dumped them in the washer. Then I turned the water temperature up to high. I used a lot of soap, too. Better safe than sorry.

CHAPTER 10

I was just coming back upstairs with my clean clothes when the doorbell rang. It was Alexei. I snapped the lock open. Gran came out of the kitchen.

"It's for me," I said.

"Kat girl!" Alexei said. "I have message. From Pavel."

"You want to come in?" I said. I looked behind me. Gran was still standing there. She had her hands on her hips.

Alexei stepped inside. "You will come to the party? Now is good. Or later."

Gran's hand clutched my arm. "Let's talk to your father about this," she said. Then she took off up the stairs. "Cameron! Cameron!" she called.

Alexei's eyes darted anxiously toward the door. "She is mad at me," he said. "I should leave?"

"No!" I said. "Don't. Please don't."

Dad's footsteps thumped down from the attic to the second floor, then down again to the first. Gran, who was right behind him, was breathing hard.

"So, what's this?" Dad said, smiling. "A party?"

"Underage drinking," Gran said. "And who knows

what else." She stomped back into the kitchen.

Dad turned to me. "Kat, I don't think—"

"Party is bad idea," Alexei said. "You wish to take a walk in the snow?"

Dad opened the door, then shut it again, quickly. It was sleeting out there—sleet on a slant, from the wind. When I looked out the little window, three girls and two guys were cutting across the road, sliding on the ice, heading toward Pavel's. They stamped their feet, coming up on the porch, and when the door opened, we heard music and laughter.

I just love parties. I raised my eyebrows at Dad. "Just for an hour?" I said.

He shook his head. No party. "Come in, son," he said. "Take your coat off. Stay awhile. Unless you're anxious to get back."

"It is a stupid party," Alexei said. Then he turned to me. "You wish me to stay? You wish to help me translate my poem?"

"A poem? You wrote a poem?"

"In my country, everyone is a poet."

We sat at the dining room table, side by side, papers and pens in front of us.

"First, I will write it in my language," he said.

I watched him, fascinated. The letters were different. I thought about little kids across the world, learning to trace those letters instead of ours.

There was more noise from the street, more laughter. Music boomed through the adjoining wall.

Gran dropped something in the kitchen. Alexei didn't even notice. He just kept on writing.

"Now," he said, "I will say it in English words, and you will write them down."

He spoke slowly, telling me where each line ended. It took me a while to figure out what he wanted me to do, which was more than just write down his words. He wanted me to make them better. Then it took him a while to read what I'd written. "It is good English?" he kept saying. "It is a good poem?"

"Yes," I said.

DREAMS

A hawk soars over the trees.
My father lights his pipe
sheltering the match with his hand.
The back wall of the house
is still warm from the sun
but the wind is from the north
and strong.

Planes shriek through the sky
then vanish
leaving only wind and clouds.

My country is sick with hatred.
My dreams are red with blood
black with smoke.

Hawks circle above me
then dive.

"It scares me," I said. "The blood and the smoke
and everything."

He nodded. His face looked sad.

"Did you come over here by yourself, or what?" I said.

He smiled, showing all his teeth. "I came with
my friend, Yuri," he said. "He is in Timmins, with
his Auntie Tatyana."

Dad came downstairs. "You guys want to come
to the video store?"

"You go," I said. Dad's a great video picker.

Gran went to the door with him, then into the
front room, to look out the window, probably, checking to see if anybody else was going to the party.

We translated one more poem, a really short one
about a tank blowing up, then Gran called the
police about the noise. We watched out the windows,
running from the front to the back so we wouldn't
miss anything.

The cruiser crept up the slippery street and
parked in front of Pavel's. When the police officers
banged on the front door, the music stopped and
people tumbled down the back steps, sharing coats
and laughing like crazy. Some of the girls fell on
the ice. After the police left, everybody went back
inside and the music started up again, only this

time it wasn't so loud.

Dad came home with two videos. The first was about the Russian Revolution. There was a lot of war stuff in it, but it was also a love story. The country parts reminded me of Heron Lake, only they didn't have cars, they had horses. In the winter the horses pulled sleds. When it was over, we made popcorn, then watched a comedy about a guy who saved stolen dogs. Dad kept rocking forward in his chair, slapping the tops of his legs, laughing so hard he was crying. We all were.

The party broke up at two-thirty. People were sliding in the street, yelling back and forth to each other. Somebody started smashing bottles. A girl screamed. When everything was quiet, Alexei went home. Before he left, he kissed me on the cheek, right in front of everybody.

Dear Suze,
I'm in love!!! Alexei came over tonight to invite me to this party at Pavel's. I couldn't go, of course (Gran went into WITCH mode about it) but (you will not believe this!) Alexei didn't go, either! He stayed here. With me. We spent, like, two hours working on these poems he wrote, translating them into English, but when they were done, we were both really happy with them. Even Gran liked them. The greatest part was that I felt

older the whole time he was here, not like a kid at all. And I just KNOW he likes me. For one thing, he had his hand on my knee half the night (under the tablecloth) and for another, he kissed me, right in front of everybody, when he left. I feel wonderful!!! All excited and tingly and, I don't know, sort of like I've been half-dead ever since we moved here, only now I'm ALIVE.

I wish you were here. I really need to talk. He's pretty funny sometimes, and very sexy, but sometimes I get the feeling he isn't sincere. Actually, he kind of reminds me of Kenny Ricken, only Alexei is sort of sad sometimes. He had to leave his country because of a war, and he misses it, which I understand completely, because I miss my country, too.

Love ya,
Kat.

CHAPTER 11

Danielle was sick. Instead of coming to the cafeteria for lunch, she went home. Erin was edgy. Sarita was polite. Neither of them had a lot to say. Desperate, I started babbling on about the first thing that came into my mind, which was homework.

"I've never worked so hard in my life!" I said. "I'm doing about four hours a night."

"I do at least five," Sarita said. "By the time I'm finished, I'm drained."

"Five hours?" Erin said. "You have five hours a night to do homework? Don't you have to work or help your mother, or look after a bunch of little kids or anything?"

Sarita's eyes were cold. "I'm the only child," she said. "There's nothing wrong with that, Erin. It's not exactly a crime!"

Tension hung between them. I turned to Sarita.

"I know for a fact you don't do homework all the time," I said, smiling, teasing her a little. "You listen to music, for one thing, and I distinctly remember you telling us how your favorite thing ever was shopping for clothes with your mom. And what about last Saturday? You hung out with us for a good two hours."

Sarita waved it away, as if music and shopping and hanging out were a total waste of time.

"You never goof off?" I pushed. "You never do stuff that's..." I was going to say normal, but that seemed a little harsh. "Don't you want to meet guys? Don't you want a boyfriend?"

Erin snorted so hard she almost choked. "Boyfriends!" she sputtered. "I'll tell you about boyfriends. They only want one thing. If you don't give it to them, they act like there's something wrong with you! If you do give it to them, they tell everybody!"

I was shocked. Sarita exploded.

"It doesn't have to be like that!" she cried. "It doesn't! I've known lots of girls with boyfriends, really nice ones. I mean, some guys might be like that, but not all of them. No way!"

Erin leaned across the table. "I'm telling you about my life," she said. "If you don't believe me, that's your problem." She stood, snatched at her backpack, heaved it over her shoulder, then turned for one last biting comment. "I just can't communicate with people like you," she said. "Spoiled little rich girls. Little princesses."

She swung away from us, then cut across the cafeteria.

"What did I do?" Sarita wailed. "I didn't mean—"

"She wanted to be mad," I said. "She was working herself up to it the whole time."

Sarita's face crumpled. "I can't do this any more," she said. "This lunch thing."

"You don't want to come anymore?" I said.

She looked away from me. "It's not you, or Danielle, it's...her. She drives me crazy."

After my last class, I dragged myself downstairs to Erin's locker, hoping I could patch things up.

She was heaving books around like she wanted to shove them through the wall. Or shove me through the wall.

"You talked about me," she said. "Don't try to tell me you didn't, because I won't believe you."

"Sarita didn't understand what she'd done, that's all."

"You just don't get it, do you?"

I shrugged. "I guess not. I'm trying, but—"

Her eyes were blinking hard. "You and Sarita. And Danielle. You have everything. I have zip," she said. "Just myself."

"You could have friends," I said. "If you didn't keep trashing them."

I got three wrong numbers before I got through to Danielle's; then I got her brother. The phone clunked when he put it down.

"Dani?" he said. "It's Kat." He spoke like she was right there, right in the same room with him, and when he came back on the line, he almost fooled me. "This is Danielle," he said.

"It is not. You're her brother."

"How did you know?"

I laughed. "Can I speak to her?" I said. "Please?"

"For sure. No sweat. Dani!" he hollered. "Phone!"

She wasn't in the room. She took too long to come. "Sorry about that," she said. "What's happening?"

"I hope you're feeling better," I said. "Because what I have to tell you is going to make you feel worse."

"Uh-oh," she said.

"Sarita doesn't want to come to lunch anymore."

"What happened?"

"Erin went on this rampage," I said. "We're spoiled little rich girls. We have everything. She has zip."

Danielle groaned. "Why?"

"We were talking about homework," I said. "About how much we're doing. Sarita does about five hours, and she was complaining about it. Well, I was complaining too. I mean, I started the complaining. Actually, now that I think about it, it was what Erin said about guys that caused the worst problem."

"What guys?"

"Boyfriends," I said. Then I explained.

Danielle gasped. "Poor Erin," she said.

"Poor us! I like Sarita."

"We'd better meet," Danielle said. "The three of us. What about Saturday? Here, at my place."

"I don't think Sarita will come. She was pretty bummed out."

"I'll make her," Danielle said. "I'll guilt her into it."

It was eleven when I went to bed; then I just lay there, thinking.

Was Erin right? Was I spoiled? I didn't get everything I wanted, that was for sure. I'd had to move, for one thing. And for another, the last time I'd asked for new clothes, Dad had just laughed at me. I'd gotten nowhere with that, but nowhere. And I did my own laundry and all the shoveling, which had been major, and I helped Gran with the cooking, so I wasn't a total sponge or anything.

I wasn't even sleepy. I just kept going over and over all this stuff in my head, replaying conversations: everything I said, everything Erin said, everything Sarita said. What I should have said, but didn't. Finally, I got up and went downstairs.

Dad was watching the news with Gran. I made myself a peanut-butter-and-jam sandwich, then headed for the attic.

Mom was staring into the computer monitor, running her fingers through her hair.

"Are you my mother?" I said.

She winced, worked a few keys, then switched

the machine off.

"Give me a bite of that sandwich, and I'll tell you," she said.

I gave her half of what was left. She moved to one end of the couch and patted the cushion beside her. I tucked my feet under her legs.

"What's happening?" she said. "Weren't you having lunch with your friends today?"

"Yeah," I said. "It was the lunch from hell." Then I described it, blow by blow.

"Poor Erin. Being here, seeing how you live, that probably set her off. In her eyes, you must seem to have everything." She grinned wickedly. "Exceptional parents, a warm and caring home, lovely clothes, enough money..."

I slit my eyes at her. "I don't know what will happen now. What if Erin doesn't come back here for her bath and everything? Where will she go? And what if she does come back? How will I deal with that?"

Mom yawned. "If you want her to keep coming, you should tell her."

I yawned, too. "I don't want Sarita to quit having lunch with us, either. She's fun, and she's lived in all these other places. She's good at school, too. Really good."

"Things will work out," Mom said. "One way or another. Maybe Erin will decide it's time to move on."

"You think so?"

Mom raised her eyebrows. "She can't communicate with you. That sounds rather final to me."

I looked at her. "I'm not sure I want that to happen, either."

There was a quilt folded on the back of the couch. Suze and I used to lie on it in our backyard, playing with our Barbie dolls. Mom shook it open and tucked it around us.

"Erin's smart, too," I said. "And she has good ideas. I mean, I have two new friends because of her. And I feel sorry for her. She's just so...difficult."

Mom nodded. "Is she difficult with everyone?"

I thought about that. "Sarita sets her off, but I think I do, too. I'm not really mean to her or anything, but I'm not really nice either."

"So you aren't perfect," Mom said. "Join the club."

"You don't understand," I said. "It was the same with that Brenda girl at home."

"The one who dropped out of school?"

"Yeah," I said. "I didn't know her that well, though."

"The only people you knew well were Suze and Tyler."

I hadn't thought about that before, but it was true.

"Anyway," I said. "Brenda was really nice and everything, but she didn't have good clothes, and stuff. I mean, she looked really rough. But when you talked to her, you knew she wasn't. Then she started going out with this guy, Kenny Ricken."

"The one Suze—"

"Yeah. And pretty soon there were rumors. Like, Brenda was, you know, a tramp."

"Ouch," Mom said. "Horrible word."

"And then she dropped out of school. And somebody said she'd run away from home and nobody knew where she was. Stuff like that."

Mom nodded. I thought she'd be shocked, but she wasn't, she just looked sad. "How does this relate to Erin?" she asked.

"I'm not sure," I said. "But after, when Brenda had dropped out, I sort of wished I'd just said something nice to her or something, only then it was too late. Like, I didn't even know where she lived, except it was out in the country, someplace. Probably it wouldn't have helped, but I felt bad. And now, with Erin, I feel bad about that, too. I mean, what I said to her today was something hard."

"Such as?"

I'd never, ever, talked to Mom like this before, never told her the bad stuff. And the weird thing was it was easy. She wasn't even mad at me.

"I went down to her locker, afterward. When she said how alone she was, and all, I told her she could have friends, if she didn't keep trashing them. I was mad when I said it."

Mom yawned. "That's not so bad. And it has the advantage of being true," she said.

I nodded.

"Getting along with people is tough," she said.

We sat there for a while, not even talking. Then Mom went to have her shower. I was waiting for her when she came out.

"How did you know about Suze and Kenny Ricken?" I said.

A tiny smile tickled the ends of her mouth. "I was surprised when you let that slip by," she said. "Sam told your father."

Sam is the Ontario Provincial Police officer who came out of the woods, the night of the big beach party, with Suze on one side of him and Kenny on the other. If anybody knew what happened that night (other than Suze and Kenny), it was Sam.

"Were Suze and Kenny, like—?"

Mom's mouth went down this time. "Yup," she said. "You didn't know?"

"She told me nothing happened," I said.

I sat there for a little while, thinking. "She lied to me," I said.

Mom was dozing on the couch, so I went back to bed, but sleep still wasn't happening. It was Suze I was all churned up about now.

I got up again.

Dear Suze,
Mom said that Dad said that on the night of the big party, Sam saw you and Kenny doing

it in the woods.
You want to comment on that, or what?

Kat

I sent it the next morning. Snail mail again.

CHAPTER 12

I t was Saturday, so I didn't have to get up. But the sun was pouring in my window, and delicious smells were wafting up from the kitchen. I rolled out of bed, then headed downstairs.

Gran was standing at the stove, flipping pancakes, but she wasn't alone.

Sometimes eavesdropping is irresistible.

"So then she got really sick," Erin said, "and she couldn't look after me anymore."

"And your father?" Gran asked. "Is he in the picture?"

"He was some lawyer she worked for. She never told me his name. I don't think he even knows I exist."

I pushed the kitchen door open. Erin was sitting at the table, an almost-empty plate in front of her. I sat across from her, rubbed the sleep out of my eyes and looked down at my pajamas, the old ones that used to be pink. "Didn't know we had company," I mumbled.

She flushed. "I came in early to use the shower," she said. "And the laundry."

"Sure," I said. I heard my voice, and it was not friendly. I tried again. "Your hair looks great," I added.

"I clean up good," she said.

Gran turned her head. "Erin will be leaving some of her things here."

Erin laughed. "Superlocker," she said.

"Cool," I said. "Are you making my breakfast too, Gran?"

"I am," Gran said. She passed me a perfect plate: three thick blueberry pancakes swimming in maple syrup, with a fat pat of butter on top. It was a bribe, a be-nice-to-Erin bribe, and I took it; but I was not thrilled, and Gran knew it.

She gave the stove one last wipe. "Now," she said. "I'm going up to get dressed. I'll only be a minute." She gave me one of her significant looks, like she was telling me something. Be nice to Erin, again, probably.

The minute Gran left, Erin took off for the basement. When she came back, she was lugging a fat green garbage bag. She dumped it on the floor by the back door, then she gave me this really sour, really bitter look.

"I don't know why you're so mad," I said. "Whatever we did, we weren't trashing you. Not like you did to us."

She glared at me. I tried again.

"It's good you have a place to leave your stuff and do your laundry, and everything. I mean, I'm okay with that. In case you were wondering."

She was standing in front of the sink, staring at

me like I was her worst enemy. I gave up. I picked up the newspaper and pretended to read.

When Gran came back, she and Erin went out in the car. They didn't say where they were going, and I didn't ask.

Good old Erin, I thought. You had to admire her, wangling her way into my space like that. Good old mysterious Erin. Score one for Erin, zero for Kat.

Two hours later, Gran came back alone. I was still in the kitchen, only now I was dressed and I was really reading the newspaper. Gran filled the kettle and set it on the stove. "We went to visit Marion," she said.

"You and Erin? You never take me."

"Marion's arthritis is worse," she said. "If she's going to be able to stay in her house, she needs help. And Erin needs a place to live. I left them together. They're talking."

I breathed a sigh of relief. I had begun to wonder if Gran was planning to move Erin in with us.

"They're both fairly skeptical, I think," Gran said. "Cautious," she added.

"How come?"

"Marion's worried about having someone she doesn't know in the house and—"

I was shocked. "You think Erin would steal stuff?"

"I don't know," she said. "Desperate people can do desperate things."

I shook my head. "What's Erin worried about?

You'd think she'd be glad to have such a nice place to stay. And Marion's so great, and—"

Gran shrugged. "Losing her independence. Being accountable to someone."

All this analysis stuff was too deep for me. I picked up the paper again. The comics here were awesome.

Danielle's house was bigger than Gran's and a lot more cheerful, but it wasn't anywhere near as tidy. Books and magazines were piled on tables and a stack of newspapers covered one cushion of the couch. In the corner by the door, three music stands were arranged around the piano. Two violins lay on a table by the window, and a clarinet, in pieces, lay in its case.

I'd expected Mrs. Vincent to be kind of thin and pinched-looking from all the worrying she did about Danielle, but I was wrong. She was heavy, with a round, glowing kind of face. It was Mr. Vincent who was skinny. He had a long, gangly body, laugh lines around his eyes, and crinkly hair with a bald patch in front.

When Sarita came, we went upstairs to Danielle's room. Except for the fat brown-and-white spaniel lying on her bed, it was immaculate.

Danielle patted him on the head. "Poor old Maurice," she said. "He's old and he smells, and he loves it here, but he's not allowed. Off, Maurice! Off!"

Maurice moved reluctantly to the floor, then pricked up his ears, pointed his nose toward the door and quivered.

Danielle put her finger to her lips, tiptoed across the room and flung the door open. "You sneak!" she roared. "You weasel! What were you planning to do, sit there all afternoon and listen?"

The guy who deked his way around her to get into the room was taller than Danielle and broader in the shoulders. He had dreadlocks instead of cornrows, but his face was almost exactly like hers. He raised his eyebrows at us and smiled a mischievous smile.

"This sorry creature is Jean Paul, my pathetic eavesdropping brother," she said. "My little brother."

"Little!" I said.

Jean Paul laughed. "She never told you about me, did she? She never tells anybody. You'd think she was ashamed or something."

"She told us she had a brother!" Sarita said.

"I bet she didn't tell you we're twins. She didn't, did she?" He threw one arm around Danielle's neck, did something complicated with her right arm and dropped her to the floor.

She retaliated with a vicious kick to his ankle. "You idiot!" she yelled. "You're not supposed to do that. You could have broken my neck." She staggered toward the bed and collapsed against the headboard.

I was half sitting on the bed, too, one leg folded

under me, the other on the rug. Sarita moved her chair closer and propped her feet between us.

"Twins!" she said. "I'd love to have a twin."

"Oh, no, you wouldn't," Danielle said. "Not a twin brother! I mean, how immature can you get? Hanging around your sister's door and listening!"

Jean Paul squatted on the rug beneath me and clasped my foot in his hands. "See how abused I am?" he said. "See how mean she is? Will you be my friend?"

I wiggled my foot away and burst out laughing.

"Get out," Danielle said.

"Why?"

Danielle rolled her eyes. "We have to talk," she said.

"I talk. I'm smart. I'm sensitive." He lay back on the rug, his foot just touching mine. "How can you discuss anything important without a male viewpoint?"

"Easily," Danielle said. "Leave! And take the dog with you."

Jean Paul sprung to his feet. "Sure," he said. "Why didn't you say so?" He flashed Sarita and me a wicked grin and stumbled out the door, crashing his shoulder into the wall as he went. He didn't take the dog.

"Sorry," Danielle said. "He has no friends yet, and he's going nuts. She flung herself off the bed, perched on the edge of her desk and sighed. "I wish we could just hang out," she said. "I wish we didn't have to get into all this heavy stuff about Erin."

Sarita shivered. "She just hates me, you know," she said. "I hardly said anything, and she jumped all over me."

"She's envious," Danielle said.

Sarita blew air out of her mouth. "Of me?" she said. "But she's so pretty! If she'd fix herself up..."

"It's you she wants to be like," Danielle said. "Your clothes, your grades—"

"And *my* family," I said. "You won't believe what's been going on. Last Saturday, after we went to the coffee shop, she came home with me. She wanted to have a shower. Then Gran suggested she do some laundry, and then she invited her for supper. Then this morning, she was there again, before I even got up. Eating breakfast, like she owned the place. And she's storing her stuff with us."

"Wow," Danielle said. "That's heavy. What are you going to do?"

I was playing with the fringe on the bedspread, making a three-strand braid, then a four-strand, then a five. "What can I do?" I said. "It's Gran's house. Anyway, it might get better. She went over to see one of Gran's friends about staying there."

"Maybe she'll be nicer if she has a good place to live," Danielle said.

"She needs to be nicer," I said. I slipped off the bed, lay on the rug, hooked my feet under Danielle's dresser and did ten bent-knee sit-ups.

Sarita moved to my spot on the bed. "So, you both

feel the same?" she said. "It's not just me? I was feeling so awful, like everything was all my fault."

I collapsed onto the rug. "Are you kidding?" I
said. "I wish I'd never brought her home. I wish I'd
never even mentioned her. The minute I did, Gran
got all interested. I mean, Erin was sucking up to
my grandmother before they even met!"

"I feel sorry for her though," Danielle said. "I
don't love her or anything, but it wouldn't be fair to
just dump her. I wouldn't know either of you, if it
wasn't for her."

Sarita's voice was sharp. "She brought us
together because she needs friends," she said. "It
was for her, not us!" Then she sighed. "When I say
stuff like that, I feel even worse, like I'm just what
she said I was—a spoiled princess."

I moved, so I was sitting with my back against
the wall. "I feel bad too," I said. "I mean, I was trying
to be nice to her this morning, trying to communicate,
but she just kept giving me these hate stares."

"We should talk to her," Danielle said. "We
should explain how we feel. That we don't like getting trashed."

I sighed. "I tried that already."

"No way I'm going to talk to her!" Sarita said. "I was
so upset after that lunch! Then my mother got upset,
and started giving me a hard time and—" She reached
for a small bottle of bright green nail polish that
stood on Danielle's desk and raised her eyebrows.

Danielle nodded. "Kat and I'll talk to her," she said. "Right, Kat?"

"I guess," I said. "You know what will happen though. No matter how nice we are, or what we say, she'll get all insulted, and then she'll stomp off again."

"She'll blame me," Sarita said, holding her painted thumbnail out in front of her, admiring it. "Then she'll hate me even more."

"You're both so pessimistic!" Danielle said. "We have to try. And I mean all of us, including you, Sarita. You don't have to talk if you don't want to, but you should be there."

"Maybe Erin won't show," I said. "Remember how she said she couldn't communicate with us? Well, I talked to my mom about that, and she said maybe Erin was dumping us."

"Maybe she is," Danielle said, "but we still have to try. So, will I do it? Will I ask her to meet us?"

I nodded. "What if she doesn't come?" I said.

Danielle shrugged, reached for the top drawer of her desk and pulled it open. "Then she doesn't. Let's all do our nails," she said. "I've got blue, too."

CHAPTER 13

Saturday night I had a video, one I chose myself, because everybody else was going out. I was just getting into it when the doorbell rang.

"I can come in?" Alexei said. "It is okay?"

"Sure," I said. "I guess." It wasn't like I was bringing a total stranger into the house. It wasn't like we didn't know him.

He flicked his eyes down the hall and began unzipping his jacket.

"I'll make tea," I said. "Then I'll tell you my troubles."

He hung his jacket and scarf on a hook in the vestibule. "Troubles?" he said. "You want me to scare somebody? Beat him up?"

"No! It's not like that. It's this girl. She's being a pain. It's not a big deal."

He draped his harm around my shoulders and rubbed his cheek against mine. "It is hard to know what to do, yes?"

"You have a beard," I said.

He raised one eyebrow. "Of course. I am a man." He jerked his head toward the stairs. "Grandmother? Mother? Father? They are...?"

"Out," I said. "Did you bring another poem?"

He smiled and looked at the floor. "We can sit in the front room? It is nice there."

"Sure," I said.

I took one end of the couch. He took the middle, then stretched his arms toward the ceiling. When they came down again, one of them was around my shoulders.

He looked into my face, to see how I was taking the arm bit, I guess. I smiled up at him. I was taking it just fine.

He moved his head so his face was touching mine. I closed my eyes, then opened them, but just a little. People look different up close. He had freckles on his cheeks, and neat, small ears. I touched them. They were sweet, like little shells.

His fingers traced my eyebrows, then my cheekbones, then the edges of my lips. He was touching me the way you'd touch a baby's face, or the petal of a flower.

He lifted my hair high off my neck and took little smoochy nibbles of skin, leaving wet spots behind. A shiver slid down my back, then another. They felt delicious.

Our first kisses were as soft as butterfly wings. Then they got deeper and longer, and his hand started moving up and down my arm, caressing it. I put my hand on his arm, too, and we stayed like that for a long time, hardly moving at all. I was so happy I could have cried. I loved being with him like that, absolutely loved it. Then his fingers started walking, across to my waist, then up under my sweater. I captured them and held them down.

That's when everything got weird. His breath got all rough like he'd just run a marathon, and his mouth pressed so hard against my teeth I was almost biting my own lip. His hand snuck up under my sweater again, only this time I could hardly hold it back. Then both his hands were there, on the waistband of my jeans, on the button. I spun away from him, and pulled my sweater down, hard.

"Shh," he said. "Relax. Everything will be nice. You will be surprised how nice it will be."

"No!" I said. "I don't want this, Alexei. I'm not—"

He looked right into my face. "Little Kat," he said. "Little baby. Too innocent for love, too young."

I groaned. "I need to think," I said.

"Ah! First you say no, now you say maybe!" He drew me toward him, rubbing his hands up and down my back. Low on my back, embarrassingly low. I shifted sideways, to get away. He followed.

"Soon you will say yes, yes?" he said. He pressed his body into mine.

I forced my arm between us. "No!" I said. "I can't! I mean, maybe someday, but—"

He leapt to his feet, then stood there, looming over me. "No? Maybe? Someday?" His face was cold and his voice was furious. "You are telling me opposite things! You are playing a game with me!"

"No!" I cried. I held my hands out toward him.
"I'm—I'm just confused...I don't do stuff like this,
Alexei!"

Tears dripped down my cheeks. I didn't want
him to see, so I buried my face in one of Gran's
cushions, the one with the tiny pink rosebuds on it.

His footsteps moved smartly across the room.
Then he yelled something I didn't understand; but
from the tone of his voice, I got the feeling it wasn't
a compliment. The outside door opened, then
banged shut, and he was gone. No kiss, no nice
words, nothing. I threw myself full-length on the
couch and cried my eyes out.

I spent the rest of the night in my room, with a
headache. That's what I told Mom and Dad when
they came home, and it was true. If you cry long
enough, you'll get one.

Mostly I was trying to figure out what had happened—how Alexei could be so sweet one minute
and then so mean the next. I had thought having a
boyfriend was supposed to be nice! You walk home
from school together holding hands, and then you
make cocoa and help each other with your homework, and when nobody's looking, you kiss. How
could he have just turned on me like that, spoiling
everything? And then act like I'd committed murder,

just because I'd said no.

I needed Suze so much! I even considered phoning her and paying for it out of my own money, but I didn't have the nerve. Not after the snotty message I'd sent. You can't more or less accuse your best friend of lying, then the minute you have a problem, call her up and start blubbering.

And there was no one else to tell. Sarita would not understand. Danielle might, but what would she think of me? The person I really wanted to talk to was Alexei. I wanted him to put his arms around me and kiss me and tell me everything was all right. I wanted him to say he wasn't mad at me any more. He needed a girlfriend, I knew that. The first time we met, out by the garage, Pavel had said so. Alexei needs a girlfriend real bad, he'd said.

The truth hit me like a baseball on the head. For Pavel and Alexei, a girlfriend was somebody you have sex with. Alexei didn't care about me at all; I was just handy. Convenient. Right next door.

Then I thought about something even worse. Some guys are really cruel, the way they talk about girls. What if Alexei was like that? What if he told Pavel everything that had happened? And Pavel told everybody else?

Sunday morning I was not my most cheerful self. I'd hardly slept, for one thing, and I was totally depressed for another. Then Gran started pressuring me. She wanted me to go to Marion's with her.

"You're drooping," she said. "It will do you good to get out of the house."

I rinsed my mug under the tap and yawned. "I'm so tired, Gran," I said. "I mean, I like Marion and everything, but..."

"We'll only stay an hour," she said. "Marion needs cheering up. And see what you can do about that long face."

Gran was right, Marion did need cheering up. She looked sad. She didn't even make the tea. She let Gran do it.

Marion's knees had been hurting her for as long as I could remember, but now her hands were bad too, so bad she could hardly do anything. She was talking about moving into one of those assisted-living places.

I sort of drifted off for a while, not really listening to the conversation, thinking about Alexei, feeling miserable. One thing that sort of bothered me was how, when he first came in the door, he'd asked where everybody was, like he was checking to make sure they were all out. Like he'd planned what he was going to do, ahead of time.

When I started listening again, the conversation had moved on. Now they were talking about Marion moving in with us. Gran wanted it, Marion didn't.

The thought of being a burden to other people
flipped her right out. "And besides," she said, "you
don't have room."

Gran sighed loudly, like she was talking to a
stubborn child. "I told you," she said. "We'll put an
addition on the back of the house. You still haven't
heard from Erin?"

Marion shook her head, then they both looked
at me.

"She never came back to do her laundry or anything?" I said. "She didn't leave her stuff?"

Gran shook her head.

"And she didn't get back to me about staying
here," Marion said.

"I'll talk to her," I said.

The minute I got home, the minute I was in the
door, I headed for my room. Then I backtracked. If I
was going to hole up, I'd need my homework. That's
when I heard Mom and Gran talking. I was leaning
on the second-floor stair railing. They were in the
front room. I couldn't see them and they couldn't
see me, but I could hear every word.

"He's a nice enough boy," Gran said, "And he's
obviously been through a lot, but he's much too old
for her. And he was here again, you know. Last
night. He left his scarf."

"While we were out?" Mom said. "She had a boy
in here while we were out?"

"She did, indeed," Gran said. "Though I'm not

saying she snuck him in."

"You don't think he'd...?"

"I wouldn't trust him as far as I could throw him," Gran said. "He's got that look in his eye. You know that look, Janet. It's a dead giveaway."

"Oh Zoe, I don't know," Mom said. "He's from a different culture. It would be easy to misinterpret—"

"One horny adolescent male is the same as another," Gran said. "No matter where they come from."

"I do worry about her," Mom said.

"The move's been hard on her. She hasn't developed any real friends."

"I thought she had!" Mom said. "There were some girls here last week! She even went to see one of them. That was just yesterday!"

"Apparently they don't measure up to Suze," Gran said.

Mom sighed. "Poor Suze. There's an accident waiting to happen, if I ever saw one."

"Kat thinks the sun rises and sets on her."

I didn't even think about what I was doing; I just marched down those stairs and blasted them. "Nothing happened with Alexei!" I cried. "Nothing! And I didn't sneak him in, he just came! And Suze isn't an accident waiting to happen! She made one mistake, one, and you're trying to make her into some kind of major loser. And she isn't! You're the losers! You're pathetic, that's what you are. Pathetic excuses for human beings! And horrible, and cruel, and mean, and awful!"

I slammed the glass doors on my way out, first one and then the other. Unfortunately, neither of them broke. I slammed my bedroom door, too, slammed it so hard the house shook. It felt so good, I did it again, and then I locked it. Nobody was going to get that door open, not ever, not unless they took the hinges off.

Dad pounded down the attic stairs, stood for a moment outside my room, then knocked.

"Kat?" he said. "What's going on?"

I ignored him. I ignored Mom, too, and Gran. They deserved to be ignored. Adults don't understand anything!

The problem with tantrums is what comes after. You can't stay in your room forever. Little details like meals and trips to the bathroom and going to school get in the way. So you have to apologize, even if it's the last thing on this earth you want to do. Even if you're not one bit sorry. Even if you figure they deserved every word you said.

Maybe, just maybe, they were right about Alexei, but they were dead wrong about me. The way they were carrying on you'd think I was some kind of brainless nitwit, and that hurt. The kind of brainless nitwit who would ignore what happened on Saturday. Who would march right up to Alexei, flash her eyes, smile a long, slow, seductive smile and...

Well, that kind of brainlessness is just plain embarrassing. I don't have the right nitwit genes.

So I apologized to Mom, and then I apologized to Gran, and then I apologized to Dad. Sweetly. Biting my tongue the whole time. That's how I got back at them. I did the right thing, but inside, I was thinking some really bitter thoughts.

CHAPTER 14

"She's not coming," Danielle said. "She would have been here by now." Lunch period was half over, but there was still no sign of Erin. Waiting for her had been tense. All we could talk about was what we were going to say when she came. If she came.

"'We're sorry' has to be part of it," Danielle said. "We're sorry if we hurt her feelings. We're sorry we haven't communicated better."

"We never meant to hurt her feelings," Sarita said. "I don't know why we have to be so sorry."

"It's important," Danielle said. "I talked to my dad about it last night, about how you can hurt somebody without meaning to." She raised her eyebrows. "So, we're sorry, right?"

I nodded.

"I guess," Sarita said.

"Then," Danielle said, "we have to tell her we want to try again. Only we want to do better this time."

Sarita didn't say anything. Neither did I.

"Hmm," Danielle said. "Does this mean what I think it means?"

"I guess so," Sarita said. "I just don't think trying again will make a difference." She smoothed her neat black skirt over her neat black tights. Compared to Danielle and me, who were both wearing jeans, she looked ultra smart, ultra sleek.

I'd already started collecting black clothes, so I'd look sleek too. So far, though, I only had one sweater. By the time I could afford black jeans and a black skirt and black tights, my sweater would be worn out.

"I don't know," I said. "It would be a lot less hassle without her, but, we haven't been exactly sympathetic. At least, I haven't."

Danielle looked at her watch. "Why don't we just go and find her? We have time. If we hang around her locker, she's bound to show up."

I hesitated. Erin's locker was just around the corner from Alexei's. The scene in the front room wasn't even three days old yet, and I was still feeling pretty raw. Besides, if he saw me down there, he'd think I was chasing him.

"You go," I said.

Danielle's eyes widened. "Do I sense a mystery here?" she said.

I took a deep breath. I had to tell them; I'd burst if I didn't. "I'm avoiding someone. His locker is right by hers."

"A guy!" Danielle said. She looked meaningfully at Sarita. "And one she's avoiding, too!"

Sarita was grinning. "Are you going to tell us

voluntarily, or do we have to pry it out of you?"

I blushed. I was losing my nerve. "It's kind of tacky," I said.

"I love tacky," Danielle said. "Tacky is the best."

Sarita leaned toward me. "You have to tell us now," she said.

I groaned, because she was right. You can't start to tell your friends something, then not finish.

"He's Pavel's cousin," I said. "You know Pavel?"

They knew Pavel.

"His name's Alexei," I said. "He lives beside us and he's eighteen and a poet and—"

"A poet?" Sarita said. "He's a brain?"

I shrugged. "I don't know," I said. "I helped him translate two poems, and we watched some movies with my parents, and it was all really nice. Then he came over on Saturday. Nobody else was at home."

"Uh-oh," Danielle said.

"Very uh-oh." The voice, coming from the large male body leaning over my shoulder, belonged to Jean Paul.

He grabbed the chair we'd saved for Erin, spun it around and straddled it. "You were saying?" he said.

Danielle shot a look at him.

He rose from his chair, about two inches. "If this is some private thing," he said. "If I've blundered into some girl thing, just tell me, and I'm out of here."

I shrugged a mini shrug, like it was no big deal. He sat down again.

"I'm completely reliable," Jean Paul said. "You can say anything in front of me. I won't get embarrassed, and I won't repeat stuff either."

"I'm embarrassed," I said. I checked out Sarita, thinking maybe she was embarrassed too, but she was busy staring at Jean Paul.

"Tell you what," he said. "I'll finish your story for you. This guy came over. Nobody else was home. He came on to you, and you—let me think about this—you said, 'Get your filthy paws off me, you animal, I'm not that kind of girl!'"

Everybody laughed, except me.

"I didn't call him an animal," I said. "I was confused, because I really like him, and then he got mad and—"

"*He* got mad!" Jean Paul said. "What did he get mad for? It's you who should have been mad!"

"He said I was playing games," I said. "And I wasn't! I was just mixed up, and upset, and..."

Jean Paul shook his head. "That's low," he said. "How do you call it, Dani? Is that low or what?"

"It's below low," she said.

Sarita made a fist and jabbed her thumb toward the floor. Jean Paul patted my arm. "He was doing a number on you."

"A guilt trip," Danielle added.

Sarita frowned. "You've been feeling bad?" she said.

I took another big breath, then let it out again. "Absolutely awful," I said.

I ran all the way home from school, partly because
I love to run and it was the first day there wasn't
ice all over the sidewalk, and partly to avoid Alexei.
When I burst through the door, Gran called out
from the kitchen.

"Letter from Suze!" she said.

I snatched it from the hall table, raced up to my
room and ripped it open.

Kat,
   I know you're mad at me, but there's a reason
I didn't tell you about Kenny, a real reason.
      When Sam found us, he hauled Kenny up
against a tree and told him if he breathed
one word of what happened, if he SULLIED
MY REPUTATION, he'd be one very sorry guy.
Sam made me promise something too. I was
to keep my mouth shut and clean up my act.
So that's what I did.
      I probably would have told you anyhow,
only just two days later your dad sprung the
news about you guys moving to Toronto. That
totally blew me away. Like, Sam told him
about me and Kenny, and whammo, you're
moving. So I wouldn't infect you, or something. I mean, how could I tell you after that,
when you were absolutely falling apart about

having to leave, and it was all my fault?

So, are we still speaking, or what?

Life here sucks. I hitched a ride to a hockey game on Wednesday, skipped school Thursday and Friday, and am seriously thinking about going out with Kenny again. Just kidding. Write to me. I miss you a lot.

Love,
Suze

At home, we had a special room for doing laundry. Here, the washer and dryer are in a dingy corner of the basement, and when you need to iron something, you have to set up the ironing board in the kitchen. After dinner, I was sitting at the table, watching Mom press shirts.

"I got a letter from Suze today," I said.

"Um hm. And what has Suze got to say for herself?"

"I asked her about Kenny. About what you said Sam said. This was the answer."

"Ah!"

"You know why she never told me? She thinks that's why we moved."

Mom tilted the big bottle of distilled water and carefully poured some into the iron, then held it up in front of her to check the little gauge that shows the water level.

"That's nonsense," she said. "We didn't move because of Suze."

"Would you have told me if we did?"

She took another shirt from a pile on the counter, laid the collar on the ironing board, and ran the iron over it. I could hear the sizzle of the steam right across the room.

"I probably wouldn't have volunteered it," she said. "But if it was true, and you'd asked, I would have told you. Of course I would."

"I miss her," I said. "I'll always miss her."

I had a mind picture of Suze, then, a picture so vivid I could almost have reached out and touched her. We were walking home from school, and she was bouncing along the sidewalk beside me, her thick honey-blonde hair shining in the sun. She was laughing and carefree and silly and she was my best friend and moving away from her was the saddest thing that had ever happened to me.

Mom hung the shirt on a wooden hanger and hooked it over the knob on the cutlery drawer. There were five other shirts hanging on different knobs, all around the kitchen. Mom never irons until she and Dad have zero clean clothes.

"You know why we moved," she said.

"I've never been all that sure. You said it was because of Gran, but then you said it was because of your new school, so..."

"Zoe was the main reason," she said. "She's getting older, and, well, finances are a problem, too."

"Gran isn't poor!" I said. "I know we paid for the renovations to the attic, but—"

"She manages," Mom said. "But only just. Look around you. The whole place needs renovations. Anyhow, it wasn't just the money. Your dad just felt he should be here. In case anything happens. We're all she's got, really."

"She has friends! What about Marion? They could live together."

Mom took another shirt from the pile and flicked a glance in my direction. "Marion has arthritis," she said.

"So? They could still live together."

"Marion can barely look after herself. If they moved in together, Zoe would end up looking after her. Then if anything happened to Zoe, there'd be two people in trouble, instead of one."

"Gran looks after her, anyway! She's over there right now! It would be a whole lot easier if they lived in the same house!"

Mom shook her head.

"It would! And it would be cheaper, too. So Gran would have more money, and we could move back home, and—"

"Don't do this, Kat," Mom said. "We're here. Cameron and I are in a great school. We'll get terrific jobs when we're through. Two good salaries, instead of one mediocre one."

She hung the last shirt on the last hanger, unplugged the iron, and held it upside down over the sink.

"How is Suze?" she said.

"She's been skipping school again. And hitching rides." I felt like a traitor, saying that, because Suze is one of the nicest people I've ever known. I've seen her bawling her eyes out because some kid she didn't even know got killed by a dog. And she wasn't just crying about the kid but about the dog, too, who had to be put down. And then there are the hours and hours she spends with her grandfather—playing cribbage, reading to him, washing his clothes, cleaning his little house. I went with her once, but I left after five minutes. She said I had a face like a prune the whole time I was there.

"You think she's missing you, so she's...acting out?" Mom said.

I shrugged. "Her mom has a new boyfriend."

"Who is it this time?"

"Arthur," I said. "The guy who runs the canteen at the beach."

"Poor Suze," Mom said.

CHAPTER 15

A big pot of tomato sauce was bubbling away on the stove, smelling wonderful. Gran was dropping elbows of macaroni into boiling water, stirring them so they wouldn't stick together. I was grating cheese.

"Alexei hasn't been around for a while," she said.

I kept my eyes on the cheese. "I thought you were mad at him."

"Because he was here when you were alone? It wasn't a good idea, and I hope you won't repeat it, but... I quite like him, actually."

I didn't say anything; I just kept on grating.

"I bumped into Pavel's mother yesterday," she said. "I wish you'd told me about Alexei's family."

"I don't know what you're talking about," I said. "What about his family?"

Gran looked over at me with big sad eyes. "He lost them."

"Lost them? Like those refugees who can't find each other? That's horrible!"

"It's worse than that," she said. "They were killed, by a bomb. That's why he left, why he came to

Canada. I'm surprised he didn't tell you."

I was surprised too, but mostly I was shocked. It was impossible to imagine anything that awful. I know people die, but your parents? Both of them at the same time? That was, like, the end. I'd be hysterical if that happened to me. Just thinking about it blew me away.

Later, when the salad was made and the casserole was in the oven, I headed up to my room. I met Dad on the stairs. He'd hardly been bugging me at all lately. I figured he'd been too busy with all his computer stuff. And he was back into sports again, too. He and Mom had been playing indoor soccer for their school. I kind of thought they might invite me to a game, but so far, they hadn't.

"How's it going, Kitten?" he said.

"Not great. Gran just told me about Alexei's family. That's so sad! And he's never even mentioned it!"

"Maybe he's not ready to talk about it," he said.

My eyes were brimming over. Dad patted me on the shoulder. I threw my arms around his neck and gave him a big hug.

"Well," he said. "Isn't this nice. We should do this more often."

I sat two tables behind Alexei in the library, so he probably didn't notice me. Later, we passed each other in the hall. He had to have seen me then, but he pretended he hadn't. I wasn't avoiding him any-more, but I got a very strong impression that he was avoiding me.

When we did meet, it was in the back lane, out by the garbage cans, each clutching a stinky little bag. I hadn't worn my coat, so I stood there, freezing, rubbing my arms with my hands, while Alexei pried the lid off the most decrepit-looking garbage can I've ever seen. Then he had to jam the lid back on again. There are raccoons in Toronto. They're even worse than in Heron Lake, so tight lids are important.

His back was turned away from me, and his voice was so low, I could barely hear him.

"I wish to apologize," he said. "You are a nice girl. I was an animal."

Usually, when somebody apologizes, you say "forget it" or "it's okay" or something, but I would never forget it and it definitely wasn't okay, so I didn't say anything. The whole scene was extraordinarily stupid: the two of us standing there, freezing to death, not even facing each other, but not going back inside, either.

Finally, I found my tongue. "Gran told me about your family," I said. "That's awful, Alexei. I feel really bad for you."

He turned toward me, pushed his jaw out and nodded. "I have a new poem," he said. "You will help me with the English?"

"Sure," I said.

After that, I started looking for chances to talk to him. I'd rush home from school, grab the shovel, and chip away at the ice covering the front walk. Or the back walk. Never seeing him either place, I figured he must be using the back entrance when I was in the front, and the front entrance when I was in the back. Or else he was going somewhere after school, and he didn't get home until we were eating dinner.

Then I started cruising by his locker when I was down there looking for Erin. I only saw him once. What I should have done was walk right up to him and start talking, but I lost my nerve. I whirled around and took off down the hall, my heart beating against my ribs so hard, the sound almost deafened me.

I didn't have much luck with Erin, either. In math, she would come in late and leave early, and because she sat at the front and I sat at the back, by the time I had worked my way out of the room, she was long gone. I saw her in the halls sometimes too, but it was always just a glimpse, and even though I'd take off after her every time, I never caught up to her. And I was too wrought up about Alexei to worry about it.

Then, late Sunday afternoon, as I was lugging my laundry through the kitchen, feeling uncomfortably bare under my jeans, Gran cornered me.

"About Erin..." she said.

I paused at the head of the basement stairs and nodded my head toward the huge, overflowing basket.

"Back in a minute," I said. "Underwear crisis."

While the first load was chugging away and Gran waited, I helped myself to an apple from a bowl on the counter, ran it under the tap and wiped it slowly and thoroughly on my sleeve. I had a bad feeling about this conversation, and it hadn't even started.

"I've tried to talk to her, Gran," I said, finally. "I try all the time, but I can't catch her. She's avoiding me."

"And why is she doing that?"

I leaned back against the fridge. "You don't have to sound so mad. It's not my fault." The way Gran looked at me, I could see she didn't believe me. "It isn't!" I said. "We aren't exactly getting along, but we invited her to lunch to talk about it, and she didn't show up."

"Why aren't you getting along?" Gran said.

I took a big bite of the apple. "Erin goes around causing offense," I said, when I finished my mouthful. "So people get offended."

"What people?"

"Sarita, mostly. But I get cheesed off too."

Gran did her little "tsk" thing with her mouth. "From what you tell me of Sarita, she doesn't strike me as a wilting flower," she said.

"You weren't there, Gran. Erin was brutal."

"Erin? Brutal?"

I took another bite. It was time to change the subject. "How's Marion doing?" I said.

"She isn't good. She needs help every day. So far, I've been doing what I can, but..." She shook her head.

"I could help," I said. "I could vacuum her house, or shovel her snow, or something."

"You'd do that? She can't pay you."

"Gran! I like her! I'm studying tonight, for a test, but I could go over tomorrow."

"You're studying?" she said.

I slit my eyes at her. "I thought I'd try it," I said. "Just for once. Just to see how it goes."

In fact, I was quite proud of my recent efforts. I've always more or less made a stab at my homework, but until we moved, I never took it all that seriously. And I certainly never studied for a test. But Sarita was sounding just a little too pompous about all her nineties. She needed competition.

"Has anybody seen Erin lately?" I said.

It was noon Monday, and we were leaning against the back wall of the school, out of the wind, our faces turned to the sun, which was getting stronger every day. Jean Paul was wearing sunglasses. So was Wing, his friend. I kept my eyes squinted, and Danielle shaded hers with her hand. I couldn't see Sarita; she was standing between Jean Paul and Wing, admiring them, probably. Sarita likes guys a lot. She doesn't come on to them or anything; she just thinks they're sweet.

"You want to see Erin?" Sarita said.

"Not particularly," I said. "But Gran found a place for her to stay, and I'm supposed to talk to her about it, only she's avoiding me."

"It's not just you," Sarita said. "I said "hi" to her the other day, and she looked right through me."

"Me too," Danielle said. "I feel kind of bad, but what can you do?"

"I have to talk to her," I said. "Gran's really bugging me about it."

Wing passed around some candied nuts. Then he began telling us about a TV program he'd watched. "It's about this guy," he said, "who goes downtown every morning at dawn, looking for birds that have flown into office towers, into the lighted windows. Saving them. I could do that. Easily."

"Aren't they dead?" Danielle said.

"Some are," Wing said. "But a lot aren't. They're just stunned. I didn't see the whole program because I had to go to Chinese school, but he puts them in little paper bags to keep them warm. Then he takes them to some place where they're nursed back to health. Is that cool, or what?"

"It's cool," Jean Paul said. "You want to go downtown some morning and find him?"

"At dawn?" Wing said. "I have a hard enough time getting up for school. If it was any other time..."

Jean Paul laughed, then everyone else did, even

Wing. Later, Jean Paul walked me to my locker.

"That guy giving you any more trouble?" he said. "The one who...?"

"Alexei," I said. "No, but I found out something."

His big, warm hand settled on my shoulder. "If he's talking about you, I'll—"

I twisted away from him. "It's nothing like that," I said. "It's something really sad. His parents got killed. Both of them. In a war. It was just before he came to Canada."

"That's rough," Jean Paul said. We were quiet for a while, just walking down the hall together, thinking our private thoughts. It was an okay kind of quiet, though, not the kind that makes you nervous.

We rounded the corner to my locker. "I can't see how that changes anything," he said. "It's not like it's an excuse for what he did."

I crouched down to undo my lock. "I don't know," I said. "Maybe it is. He said he was sorry, and he still wants me to help him with his poetry, the translation part, but..." I pulled the books for my next class onto the floor, and looked up.

He squatted beside me. "But you don't know what else he wants. Or maybe you do."

"I guess," I whispered. "The problem is, I don't know what I want." I grabbed my books, snapped the lock back on, and stood up.

Jean Paul stood up, too. "Maybe you should— nah," he said. "Never mind."

"Maybe I should do what?" I leaned against the wall. "It drives me crazy when people do that, when they start something and don't finish."

His Adam's-apple bobbed up, then down again, and his words came out in a rush, like he was embarrassed about saying them. "Maybe you should get a different boyfriend," he said. "One who won't put that kind of pressure on you."

I shook my head and started walking. He came with me.

"Not every guy is a sex maniac," he said. "I mean, they might have the feelings, but they don't try to force them on anybody."

I shrugged, and looked away.

He put his hand on my arm. "Lots of guys would be interested in you," he said. "Lots."

I wanted to move his hand away, but I didn't want to make him feel bad, so I kind of shifted around until he let go.

"You don't believe me?" he said.

I stopped walking. "You don't understand," I said. "I like him. And he's had such a hard time and everything. I think he needs me."

Jean Paul sighed, then tapped me on the hand. "Just don't do anything dumb," he said. "Just don't do anything that will wreck your life."

CHAPTER 16

A lexei stood at the door. "I have a poem," he said. "This is a convenient time for you?"

"Sure," I said. I pulled the door wide open and stepped backward.

He didn't move. "It is a very special poem," he said.

"So come in, then."

He looked at the floor of the porch and shuffled his feet.

"Is there a problem?" I said.

He nodded. "It is a problem of trust."

"You don't trust me?"

"It is a very sad poem," he said. He put his hand over his heart. "It is difficult to speak of such things. Difficult to listen, also."

I grabbed his arm and pulled him inside. We sat at the dining room table again, only this time I took the end where Gran usually sits. Alexei was on the side. We were close, but not close enough for kneesies.

"So what's the poem about?" I said. "More war stuff?"

Alexei shrugged. He was different today, quieter. Even his voice was quieter. "It is about war and it is about...family," he whispered. His face went bright pink. "About sisters."

"Sisters!" I said. "I didn't know you had sisters! How old are they?"

At first I thought he was choking, seriously choking, the kind you have to call 911 for. But when he started heaving with great, wrenching sobs, and the tears started flowing, I got the picture.

I stood behind him with my hands on his shoulders, crying with him. "Tell me," I said. "Tell me, Alexei. Please."

"Dead!" he wailed. "Mother! Father! Sisters! They were so little, so little..." He threw his arms across the table and bashed his forehead down between them. Three times, he bashed it like that. It had to be hurting.

"Tell me their names," I whispered. "Tell me your sisters' names. Tell me how old they were."

When he raised his head, his eyes were closed and his voice was flat. "Katya and Mariya," he said. "Six years and four years."

I went out to the kitchen for Kleenex, and after that I made tea. Gran was sitting at the kitchen table, quiet as a mouse, reading. When she looked up, there were tears in her eyes, too.

We worked on the poem all afternoon. Sometimes we had to stop, because we were too upset.

It started out kind of funny and nice. It was only the last bit that was awful.

Pigs
A woman scrubs a table
complains about food on the floor
and children who eat like pigs.
Then she laughs.
My little piggies, she says.

Her husband makes piggy noises.
Two small girls in blood-red nightgowns
their dark hair shining in the firelight
lie back in his arms, giggling.

Missiles scream through the night.
Walls crumble. An armchair smolders.
A table, three legs broken
lies toppled in the dirt.

"The last part is too terrible to write," Alexei
said. "It is finished. Everything is finished."
"Where were you?" I said. "When it happened."
He covered his eyes with his hands. "Out," he
said. "With Yuri."
He left then, taking his poem with him. Even
Gran didn't get to read it, I was the only one.
I went up to my room and lay on my bed and
thought about little children dying. I thought about
how awful some people's lives are. Then I thought
about what it would be like to be Alexei's girlfriend:
the way he wanted it to be, and the way I wanted it

to be, which were two entirely different things.

Three days later, I saw a very different Alexei. This
one was standing in front of the door to the library,
laughing. His thumb was hooked in the back pocket
of a girl's jeans, his long fingers splayed out over
one cheek of her bum. The girl was staring up into
his face, smiling a really wide smile, like she'd just
won the lottery.

I barely made it through the rest of the day. By
the time I burst through the door of the house, I
was bawling like a baby.

"Alexei has a girlfriend!" I wailed.

Gran came whipping down the stairs. "Oh, dear,"
she said. "Oh, dear."

I snorted, trying to hold my tears back, and
swiped at my nose with my sleeve. "He used me!"
I said. "He pretended he liked me so I'd help him
with his poem!"

"I'm sure that's not true," she said. "Perhaps you
misinterpreted? If he thinks of you as a friend—"

"I didn't misinterpret! I didn't!"

She raised her eyebrows. "You're certain of that?"

"Dead certain," I said. I charged into the
kitchen, grabbed a Kleenex and honked into it.
Finding out about Tyler and Penelope was nothing
compared to this, nothing. This was big-time hurting.

I stormed up and down the kitchen—basement
door to table, then back again. "When he told me

about his family," I said, "when he cried and everything, I thought he really liked me!"

Gran was filling the kettle from the tap. "I'm
sure he does," she said.

"I mean a different kind of liking than that, Gran."

"You thought he liked you as a girlfriend?"

"He did," I said. "Before. I'm right about this,
Gran. I mean, we did stuff."

She turned to face me. "Not...?"

"No," I said. "Not that, but..."

Gran nodded. She understood, and she didn't
make me spell it out. I was so grateful for that, I
could have hugged her, but I wasn't sure she'd be
all that thrilled about it, so I didn't.

"If I'd done what he wanted," I said. "I'd be his
girlfriend now!"

Gran put two cups beside the teapot. "Ah," she
said. "But then he came back, for help with a very
special poem, and you thought —"

I nodded. "I thought he still liked me even though
I wouldn't, you know."

For a second there, when she grinned, Gran
looked a whole lot younger. "I do know," she said.
"It was a long time ago now, but you don't forget
things like that."

I cracked a smile.

"I'm quite sure," she said, firmly, "that Alexei likes
and respects you, and trusts you, too. After all, he
shared some of his most painful memories with you."

I slid down to the floor, my back against the fridge, my knees under my chin. "He tried me out, Gran, and I flunked."

"You didn't flunk. You set limits on the relationship."

"I got the shove," I said.

She held the teapot out in front of her and nodded toward the table. I sat across from her.

"He asked and you refused. That's a very strong thing to have done."

"It is?" I said.

"I'm extremely proud of you," she said. "If you remember anything from this conversation, I hope you'll remember that."

I nodded. My neck was so stiff I thought it was going to break. I tilted my head forward, then back until I was looking at the ceiling. After that I tilted it from side to side. Then I blew my nose again. "I don't want Mom and Dad to know," I said. "I just hate it when you guys talk about me. When you discuss me. Like when Dad told you about the beach party."

Gran's mouth twitched, then widened to a grin. "I'll keep your secret," she said, "but you needn't feel bad about that party." The grin got bigger, then she laughed out loud.

"You weren't mad?" I said.

"Mad?" She shook her head. "Why would I be mad? It was the best laugh I'd had in years! One police officer," she said, chortling, "a whole beach full of kids, stark-naked, and there was my darling granddaughter..."

I screwed up my face, reliving the whole thing. The bonfire on the sand, showers of sparks shooting up to the stars. The loons calling to each other across the lake. Then somebody decided we should go skinny-dipping. That's when I got a little frantic, when everybody started stripping off. Even Suze, even Tyler. And I just couldn't do it. I got as far as my underwear, then I froze.

Gran was still kind of laughing, like everybody being naked except me was some big joke, but it wasn't.

"I felt like an idiot," I said. "But there was no way I was going to strip off, no way. What I never understood was why Dad was so furious about the whole thing. It wasn't even see-through underwear. It covered more than a bikini!"

"He wasn't furious," she said. "He was upset. About Suze."

I remembered everything about that night, every last detail, like it all happened yesterday, not seven months ago.

Coming out of the water in my underwear, getting teased, getting hassled, because I wasn't naked too. Feeling scared, like something bad could happen. Then everybody starting to pair off and disappearing into the woods, carrying blankets. Even Suze. I felt really bad about her going off with Kenny like that. She wasn't even going out with him. She didn't even like him.

"Why was Dad so upset about Suze?" I said. "He's not her father."

Gran frowned. "When he found out what she'd been up to with that Kenny character, he was afraid that you'd—"

I smacked my mug on the table. Fortunately, it was almost empty. "Well, I didn't!" I said.

"No," she said, "you didn't. But you must see how he'd feel. You did everything together. You skipped school with her, you hitched rides with her..."

"Once!" I said.

"Parents worry," she said. "There are a lot of pressures on teens."

I groaned. "Tell me about it," I said.

Snail mail
Dear Suze,
Remember Alexei, the poet guy I wrote you about, who's so cute and nice and everything? Well, he has a not-so-nice side, too. He came on to me and when I said no, he got furious and tried to make out like I was playing games, because after I said no, I said maybe, and after that, I said maybe someday. Well, he apologized and everything, so we're speaking again, but we're not going out. Then, just a few days ago I found out that his parents were killed, both of them, just

three months ago. So maybe there's a reason he was so awful, and it wasn't just me. Anyway, now he has a new girlfriend who's really beautiful and she can't keep her hands off him, and he can't keep his off her, and all I can do is pretend I don't care. But I do. Big time.

I wish you were here, so we could talk. Write soon,

Love,
Kat

P.S. Gran's friend Marion is really sick, so this week I vacuumed and dusted her house for her, for free. Brownie points!

P.P.S. I studied really hard for a science test and got eighty-two!

P.P.P.S. We moved because of Gran, and because of Mom and Dad's new school, not because of you.

CHAPTER 17

M rs. Shah's sari was printed with tiny gold leaves. Gold bracelets slid up and down her arms, and gold earrings dangled from her ears. She lifted and turned a circle of dough on a thin wire rack, which sat right on top of the hot element of the stove. The bread puffed up as it cooked, then flattened as it cooled.

"Aren't you afraid you'll burn your fingers?" I said.

She laughed. "I've been doing this since I was Sarita's age!"

Sarita was arranging dishes of food on the kitchen table: a huge platter of deep-fried vegetables; small bowls of a thick, dark soup; a larger bowl of rice. An after-school snack, she called it. Danielle and I called it a feast.

The apartment kitchen was tiny, barely big enough for the four of us, but it opened into a large L-shaped living dining room. The couches and chairs were covered with dark reds and blues and purples and shiny brass ornaments were everywhere: big round trays, vases, a great long-necked bird, a tall, thin coffee pot.

If somebody had asked me what kind of a room
Sarita would have, I would have guessed modern,
like Danielle's. I would have been half right. She
had frilly pink curtains, a deep-pink satin quilt,
and a heap of bright cushions. But a plain black
desk stood under the window, home for a color
printer and a computer to die for.

"Erin would have a fit if she saw that," I said.
"Can you imagine?"

Danielle pulled the chair out from the desk and
straddled it. "Have you seen her lately?" she said.

I shook my head, then perched on the edge of
the desk. "She missed math twice," I said. "Last
week she was avoiding me. This week she just isn't
there. Gran thinks something's happened to her. I
have to check with the office every day, to see if
they've heard anything."

Sarita stepped up onto the bed, walked across
it to the headboard, then sat cross-legged on the
cushions. "She's probably transferred to another
school," she said. "To get away from us. Because
we're so horrid. She thinks everybody's horrid.
Remember what she said about guys? I mean, was
that sick, or what?"

"It was sad," Danielle said. "She must have a
reason for thinking like that. I feel sorry for her."

Sarita shivered. "I'd love to know what really
happened to her parents. It's a different story every
time she tells it."

Danielle pulled a tiny elastic off one of her braids, rebraided the end, then put the elastic back on again. "She was in at least one foster home," she said. "But she didn't stay. Maybe she was having problems with some guy."

"Maybe she was the problem," I said. "She's not exactly the easiest person to get along with."

I looked at my nails, then waved them at Sarita. She pointed to a pink leather manicure case on her dresser. Inside it were twenty-four bottles of polish.

"Maybe that guy with the great leather jacket is her father," I said.

Danielle pushed her lips out and shook her head. "I don't think so. He's either dead or she never knew him, depending on which story you believe. Or both, I suppose." She moved closer to the manicure case, snatched the black polish just as I was reaching for it, then held it away from me, and grinned. "Wait your turn," she said. "I think that guy was a drug dealer."

"Erin doesn't do drugs!" I said. "She's never out of it. Her eyes aren't weird, she doesn't smell — "

"There's lots of different drugs," Danielle said. "You can't always tell when a person's on something. I knew a guy who was bombed out of his mind constantly, but the only reason I knew was because his brother told me."

Sarita unknotted her hair and shook it over her shoulders. "Speaking of guys," she said, "whatever happened to Alexei?"

I winced. "He got another girlfriend."

"Good!" she said. "He was too old for you, Kat. Too—"

"Sexy," Danielle said. "You could get a much nicer boyfriend, I know you could."

"I don't want another boyfriend," I said.

Later, when our nails were dry, we tried on saris. Sarita had three drawers of them. Then we showed ourselves off to Mrs. Shah. She said we looked stunning, absolutely stunning, and very grown up. Crowding in front of the long mirror behind Sarita's door, we had to agree.

I was lugging groceries from the car to the house, trying not to slip on the icy path, when Alexei came blasting out of his back door, climbed the huge snowbank in his yard, and stood on top of it.

"Wait!" he called. "I need to speak to you!"

"Speak to your girlfriend," I said, and kept walking.

"What for are you mad?" he asked. "You are my friend, yes?"

I set the groceries on the path beside me. "What kind of friend?"

He put his hand on his chest. "A friend of the heart. That is good, yes?"

I shrugged, like I'd think about it and get back to him. My brain knew better than to fall for his smooth talk, but Brainless Nitwit was definitely interested. She perked right up. I swatted her down, and put a frown in my forehead, but getting that frown to take was really tough.

"I think I know why you are mad with me," he said. "But I do not understand. You did not wish to be my girlfriend."

"Not the kind of girlfriend you want!"

His eyes looked boldly into mine. "Later, perhaps, you will change your mind?" he said.

"Alexei!"

"Why not?"

I shook my head. Brainless Nitwit pouted.

"Many girls do these things. At fourteen years, fifteen years..."

"Many girls do lots of things I don't!"

He slid down the snowbank toward me, one foot in front of the other, hopped over the fence, and laced his hand through mine. Then he kissed my fingers, one at a time.

Brainless Nitwit just loves finger kisses. I snatched my hand away. "You're a flirt!" I said. "That's what you are, a flirt."

His eyes were laughing at me. "A flirt is not serious. I am serious. Therefore, I am not a flirt."

"I'm serious, too," I said. "I'll be your friend, only you have to behave! All the time. None of this 'maybe later' stuff. It's not fair!" *And that means you, too,* I told Brainless Nitwit.

His face got serious then. "I will try," he said. He

kissed his fingers, then slowly moved them toward my mouth. I ducked, grabbed my bag of groceries and ran toward the house. Brainless was in a right snit. I had to drag her along behind me.

CHAPTER 18

G ran was really on my case about Erin, so on Monday, just before lunch, I went to the office to see if they'd heard anything. My old school had one secretary. Here there are six. The one I wanted was behind the counter, sorting through a stack of pink message slips.

"It's about that Orme kid, right?" she said.

I nodded.

"You're not the only one who wants to know," she said. "We had the police in here, asking around. She's in the hospital, in intensive care."

"The police! In the hospital?" I said. "I thought she changed schools! You're sure?"

She glared at me. "Would I joke about something like this?"

"What hospital? And why intensive care? What happened?"

"I don't know. All I know is that things are not so good for Erin Orme." She wrote the name of the hospital on another pink message slip and handed it to me. "Let us know how she is," she said.

I ran all the way home. It was pouring rain and

there were puddles everywhere. Every time I put my feet down, I splashed myself, so I was wet from the bottom up as well as from the top down.

I fanned my jacket over two hooks in the vestibule, kicked my shoes into a corner, and called out to Gran. "Erin's in the hospital!"

She flew out of the kitchen, wiping her hands on a dish towel. "What's wrong with her?"

"I don't know. I don't think the secretary knew either, but she's in intensive care." I fished the pink message slip from my backpack and handed it to her.

She called Information first, then the hospital. "Erin Orme," she said. "A patient. Can you tell me what's happened to her?"

When she hung up, her shoulders slumped and she sighed deeply. "They only give information to the family," she said. "A fat lot of good that is."

"So how do we find out—?"

"We visit her."

"We?"

"We," she said.

Visiting hours had already started by the time we got there, and all the parking lots were full. We finally found a spot three blocks away, then we walked back, huddled together under Gran's umbrella. My shoes squished. They hadn't dried out from the afternoon.

We went through the emergency entrance, because it was the closest. An ambulance pulled up just as we got there, and somebody on a stretcher was rushed inside. I kept my eyes half-shut. There are some things you don't need to see.

We waited for the elevator in a special elevator hall and when everybody crowded on, I got stuck in a corner behind a wheelchair. The guy sitting in it, who didn't look any older than me, was wearing blue striped pajamas. He had patchy bald spots on his head and patchy red spots on his face, and he smelled like he'd just upchucked his dinner. That's when I started feeling weird—going up in that elevator, jerking to a stop, jerking to a start again, looking down at that sick guy, inhaling him.

Intensive Care was on the fifth floor. Two nurses were sitting behind a high counter. One was talking on the phone. The other was writing away like her life depended on it. The phone nurse shot a look in our direction, checking us out; looking for terrorists, probably.

A guy in a purple cotton tunic and matching pants rushed past us, pushing a bed. The person on it had her eyes closed, wasn't moving, and was extremely pale. I tugged at Gran's arm.

"Is she dead?" I said.

Gran shook her head impatiently. "Sedated, maybe. Or still under anesthetic."

The hall we were in ended. You could go left to

some more rooms or right to this depressing little sitting place—four orange plastic chairs and a table with chewed-looking magazines. Gran pointed me in their direction and took off to where the Intensive Care was, so I sat there, looking around. I lifted my feet for a floorwaxer. I smiled at a guy in a striped housecoat. Visitors tiptoed into the rooms, looking sad and serious.

A woman and two men, all doctors with white coats and stethoscopes, came out of one of the rooms, then stood together in a little huddle. The woman was wearing an African-style head scarf, and a long, flowing dress under her white coat, and she was quizzing the men. She'd ask them something, then they'd look through the papers on these clipboards they had, and come up with an answer. I was really getting into watching them, when Gran came back. She'd been gone about two minutes.

"I found Intensive Care," she said. "But there's a notice on the door saying you have to push a buzzer to get in, so you'd better come with me. That way, we'll only have to bother them once."

The nurse who came to the door walked ahead of us into a big room, which was divided into smaller rooms by sliding partitions. She turned a corner and led us to somebody in a bed; somebody who looked sort of familiar, only her face was all red and purple and swollen. A mean-looking cut sliced into one of her eyebrows, and one wisp of greasy blonde hair stuck out from under a helmet of bandages.

"She's asleep?" I whispered.

"She's in a coma," the nurse said.

There were two tubes attached to her, one going in and one coming out. The going-in tube came from a bag on a pole and led into a vein in her hand. The coming-out tube came from somewhere under the covers. It was draining a pale yellow liquid into a bag pinned to the sheet.

"What happened?" Gran said.

The nurse rubbed Erin's arm. "An accident, we think. She came in by ambulance. The 911 call was anonymous."

Gran touched Erin's cheek with the tips of her fingers. "What are her chances?" she said.

The nurse looked at Gran, then at me. "She's listed as being in critical condition," she said. "When did you last see her?"

"Several weeks ago," Gran said. "She came to the house for breakfast."

"The only other visitors she's had are the police," the nurse said. "Are you in touch with her parents?"

Gran shook her head. "As far as I know, she has no one."

"If you'll stop at the desk on your way out," the nurse said, "and leave your name and phone number, we'll notify you...if there's any change."

Gran nodded.

There was one chair. When the nurse left, Gran

pulled it closer to the bed, took Erin's hand in hers and started patting it. Tears filled my eyes, then overflowed.

"Poor Erin," Gran said. "She's had an awful life, just appalling, really. But she's such a little fighter, so spunky, with such an amazing will to better herself." She peered closely into Erin's face. "I wonder," she said. "I suppose it could have been an accident, but—"

"You think somebody did that on purpose? You think somebody beat her up?"

Gran raised her eyebrows. "I hope not," she said. "It makes you think, though, doesn't it? If she'd trusted us more, she might be living with Marion now, safe and sound."

If she trusted me more. That's not what Gran said, but it's what she meant. If I was nicer. Then Erin would have come to the house more, for showers and laundry and stuff. And we could have been her superlocker.

I felt awful, beyond awful. I'd been awful. Right from the first day we met, when she almost fell down the stairs. The day she said she was obligated to me until she saved my life back.

Now I wondered if she'd get the chance.

Dear Suze,
The big news here is that Erin is in the hospital, in a coma. She just lies there looking like she's dead, only she isn't. Nobody knows

what happened, except that she got her head bashed in. She looks absolutely pathetic, all bruised and cut, with these tubes attached to her—one by a needle into the back of her hand, and I don't even want to think about where the other one goes. It makes me feel all icky.

The first time we went to see her, it was just Gran and me. Then last night we took Sarita and Danielle and it was even worse, if that's possible. Sarita started to bawl and she couldn't stop and she was so loud the nurses said we had to leave. So Danielle and Gran and I had to practically drag her out, which was a bit much seeing as how we were seriously upset too. I mean, the nurse more or less told us Erin isn't going to make it.

Anyway, we all feel pretty bad. Erin is weird, and when she's mad you really don't want to be there, but if it wasn't for her, Danielle and Sarita and I wouldn't even know each other.
Why aren't you writing? I miss you.

Love,
Kat

CHAPTER 19

Three days later, Gran, Sarita, Danielle, and I stood in front of Erin's bed, staring at the guy lying in it, then staring at each other. I know what I was thinking, and I had a pretty good idea what everybody else was thinking too. Erin hadn't made it.

"We shouldn't have just walked in after that orderly like that," Danielle said. "We should have pushed the buzzer and waited for a nurse. They may have just moved her to another bed." She beckoned me to follow her and we did a quick tour of Intensive Care. Most of the beds were full. None of them held Erin.

When we came back to where Gran and Sarita were standing, we shook our heads.

"We should ask somebody," Danielle said.

There were two nurses in the room but they were busy with a patient, a guy with a mask over his face who was having trouble breathing.

Gran took a deep intake of breath, herself. "She could be better," she said. "They could have moved her to an ordinary room."

"Sure," I said.

"If anything happened," she said, "someone would have phoned."

"Unless they forgot," I said. "Or they've been too busy. Or they lost our number." Or she just died, I thought. And they haven't got around to it yet.

We trooped out to the nursing station. Gran looked about a hundred years old. Sarita staggered, like she was going to collapse. I felt like I was in the middle of a nightmare. Only Danielle seemed to have her head together.

There was a different nurse at the desk, a big woman with a big smile.

"Erin Orme?" Danielle said. "In Intensive Care? She isn't in her bed."

"Perhaps she's been taken downstairs, for tests?"

"You don't understand," Danielle said. "Her bed isn't empty. Somebody else is in it."

The nurse's smile disappeared. She checked some files on the desk in front of her. Then she checked the intensive-care room. When she came back from there, she got on the phone. The first two places she called, nobody knew anything. Sarita was crying. I was trying not to. Gran just stood there, looking at the floor. Danielle was tapping her fingers on the counter, her eyes on the nurse's every move. After the third phone call, we got the big smile again.

"Room 504," she said. She pointed to the hall off

to her left. "Corridor J, about halfway down. She's been moved."

"They've given up on her," I said. "They've put her in there to die."

We trudged along Corridor J. It was buzzing with noise, the kind you hardly notice once you get used to it, but over and above that, there was something else: a loud, angry voice, a female voice. And the closer we got to room 504, the louder it got.

"Are you out of your pathetic little mind?" it said. "If I've told you once, I've told you a thousand times, I'm not going!"

Sarita laughed and grabbed my arm. I laughed and grabbed hers back. Danielle's face took on a luminous glow. Only Gran didn't get it.

"Gran, it's Erin!" I said. "That's her voice! She's alive! I knew she wouldn't die!"

"That's not Erin!" Gran said. "Erin wouldn't screech like that!"

"Yeah, right," I said. I whipped in front of everybody and barged into the room. There were four beds. Two of them, the ones closest to the door, had rumpled sheets, but no patients. The two near the windows were curtained off. The noise came from the one on the right.

Erin's voice was dry and rough. "Slither off, Ricardo," she said. "I've already got the headache from hell. You're making it about a trillion times worse."

I peeked through the curtains. Ricardo, an older

guy in a buttery leather jacket, wasn't giving up easily. "Erin," he said. "Use your considerable intelligence for once, will you? You can't go back to that place after this kind of injury! You need care and rest and stability."

"Nurse!" Erin yelled. "Nurse! This man is harassing me! Nurse!"

Ricardo backed out of Erin's space, and I backed away from Ricardo. A nurse bounded into the room, catching me between them. She looked at Ricardo and shook her head. Ricardo rolled his eyes, passing me as he headed for the hall. The nurse passed me too, heading in the other direction, toward Erin's cubicle. I stood there in the little passageway between the beds. Gran, Danielle, and Sarita filed in behind me.

"Now, Erin," the nurse said, "working yourself into a frenzy won't do your poor head any good at all, and it's very upsetting for Meiying."

Meiying didn't comment, but I caught a glimpse of her through a crack in her curtains. She looked upset. I'd look upset, too, if I was sick and in the hospital, and had to share a room with a Mouth.

Gran stuck her head through Erin's curtains. "Ahem!" she said.

The nurse looked relieved. "Visitors, Erin!" she said.

"Visitors suck," Erin said. "I don't care if it's the Prime Minister out there. I don't care if it's Prince William. I'm not talking to anybody!"

Gran laughed and pushed the curtains open. "What about friends?" she said. "Are we allowed?"

Erin's bed was cranked up so she was half sitting, half lying. The helmet of bandages was smaller, her face less swollen; and the purplish-red color had been replaced by greenish-yellow.

"You!" she said. "What are you doing here?"

"You never brought your things over," Gran said, "so I started fussing."

"And you weren't in math," I said.

Sarita whipped around Erin's bed to the uncrowded side. "So Kat asked about you at the school office."

"This is our third visit," I said. "The last two times you were out like a light."

The nurse left. Gran took the only chair. I leaned against the windowsill, beside Sarita. Danielle perched gingerly on the end of the bed.

Erin looked half pleased, half embarrassed, and totally sick. "I guess you heard me roaring," she said.

"Hard not to," Danielle said. "Who is that guy, anyway? The last time we saw him, you were mad at him too."

Erin made a face, then winced. "He's my worker," she said. "From Children's Aid. He wants me to go to a foster home. He always wants me to go to a foster home, only this time he's got the hospital ganging up on me, too. They won't release me until I agree. They've even taken my clothes!"

"What about going to Marion's instead?" Gran
said. "I know she's been hoping to hear from you."

"I figured that was some kind of charity thing,"
Erin said. "I figured you put her up to it."

"I certainly did not!" Gran said. "Marion's arthritis
is terrible! She's so desperate, she's been talking
about moving into a nursing home."

"You should see her, Erin, her hands," I said.
"They're all bent. She can hardly do anything."

Erin ran her tongue over a large crack in her bottom lip. "You think she'd still want me?" she said.
"I'm not a heck of a lot of good to her right now..."

"You'll get better," Gran said. "Have they told
you how long—"

"Another couple of weeks. I should live so long."

Gran put her hand on Erin's arm. "What happened, Erin? Was it an accident?"

"I got beat up," she said. "This guy kept ripping
me off and I, like, confronted him. Next thing I
know, I'm in the hospital and there's a whole
chunk missing from my life."

"What did he steal?" Sarita said.

Tears squeezed out of the corners of Erin's eyes.
"Only everything I owned," she said. "My clothes,
my backpack, my books..."

"You have no clothes?" Danielle said.

"Just what I had on. And my student card. It was
in my back pocket or he would have taken that, too."

"I have some stuff I could give you," I said.

"So do I," Sarita said.

"If you don't mind swimming in your clothes," Danielle said, "so do I."

Erin frowned. Maybe she had a headache, or maybe she really didn't like charity.

Gran edged her way down the bed, past Danielle's feet. "I'm going to find a phone and call Marion," she said, smiling. "You girls keep Erin company."

There was an awkward silence when Gran left, then everybody spoke at once, which produced another awkward silence. I broke it.

"You don't have to rest or anything?" I said. "I mean, we could go."

Erin eyeballed me. "All I do is rest. I asked for a TV, but they cost."

I looked around. Everything in that little cubicle was really plain, really boring. The view outside the window was boring too. All you could see were roofs and chimneys.

"My Walkman is in the car," I said. "I could lend it to you until you're out of here."

She didn't light up or anything, but I got the feeling she was pleased. "You'd do that?"

"Sure," I said. "I only have two tapes though. But I can bring more the next time we come."

"I thought you guys didn't like me," Erin said. "You give off these vibrations sometimes."

Sick or not, I wasn't letting her get away with that. I mean, she was right, but vibrations go two ways.

"You give off vibrations, too," I said. "Like you think we're deliberately insulting you, when we're not."

"And we asked you to come and talk to us," Danielle said. "But you didn't show up."

"I'd laugh," Erin said, "but it would hurt my face."

"It must be really sore," Sarita said. "It sure looks it."

"And your head," Danielle said. "Is it all bashed under there?"

"One bash," Erin said. "And the eyebrow slice. They gave me a mirror just before Ricardo came. I look like the backside of a baboon."

"But you're okay?" I said. "I mean, I know you hurt, but you'll get better?"

"Yeah," she said. "That's what they're telling me, so I guess I will."

"We were really scared," I said. "Coming in and all. We thought you'd still be in a coma, in that other room, and then you weren't there and they couldn't find you and — "

"We thought you were dead," Danielle said.

When Gran came back, she was still smiling. "Marion sends her love," she said. "And she renewed her invitation. She'd be absolutely delighted to have you, Erin." She rummaged around in her purse until she found a pen and a bit of paper. "But I suppose we'll have to clear it with Children's Aid. What was your worker's name, Erin? Ricardo..."

"Ricardo Lopez," Erin said, frowning. "Why?"

Gran raised her eyebrows. "I thought I'd talk to him about Marion. About what a wonderful foster mother she'd make."

Erin's eyes shifted to the window. "I've had enough foster mothers to last a lifetime."

Gran blinked.

"I'll go to Marion's," Erin said, "but no foster mother stuff. I'll stay as long as it works, but if it doesn't, I'm out of there. I just want to make sure everybody understands that."

CHAPTER 20

"Well, I don't get it," I said. "This worker guy is desperate to get Erin in a foster home, right? And the hospital people, they're desperate for the same thing. Only Erin, she isn't buying. What I can't figure out is how this is going to work."

Gran's mouth flattened; whether it was because of what I'd said or the traffic, I couldn't tell. The hospital parking lot was bumper-to-bumper cars, which is what happens when all the visitors leave at the same time.

"She'll have to go to a foster home first," she said. "Then later, when she's well enough, she can move in with Marion."

"Didn't you hear her, Gran?" I said. "She won't go to a foster home. You're still going to talk to that Ricardo guy, right?"

"I don't see the point, given Erin's feelings about foster mothers." The car crept forward, then stopped again almost immediately. "Gridlock," she said, sighing. "This is going to take a while."

"Maybe Ricardo will let her go to Marion's any-

way, even though it isn't a foster home," I said.
"You could ask. You could tell him how great she is,
and everything."

Gran sighed again. "This is something Erin will
have to sort out for herself. It's not something I
want to interfere in," she said.

I slipped my arm behind the front seat and
made circular hand motions to Sarita and Danielle.

Danielle caught on. "She won't be able to sort it
out," she said. "She'll make a run for it."

"In the buff?" Gran said.

"That won't stop Erin," Sarita said. "She'll get
some clothes. Borrow them, or..."

"You don't know her, Gran," I said. "She won't go
to a foster home, but she won't just sit there cooling
her heels in the hospital, clothes or no clothes.
She'll take off. Then she'll end up in that terrible
restaurant again, when she should be resting."

"Right," Danielle said. "Erin won't bend, the hospital won't bend. Somebody needs to get in the middle,
somebody needs to help them sort everything out."

"Someone mature," Sarita said, unsnapping her
seat belt and leaning forward, folding her arms on
the back of my seat. "Someone sensible."

Danielle unsnapped her seat belt too. "Someone
the hospital people can trust," she added.

"They'd listen to you, Gran," I said. "You could
tell them about Marion. You could even take them
to see her."

"It would be very nice if you'd do that," Sarita said.

"And extremely kind," Danielle added. "Kind to Erin."

"For heaven's sake!" Gran said. "I feel like I'm being attacked by a nest of hornets! And get those seat belts back on!"

"Oops," Danielle said. "Sorry."

"I will not get involved in this," Gran said.

"But why?" I said. "You were going to get involved before. You even wrote that guy's name down."

Gran closed her eyes and groaned. Fortunately, we still weren't moving. "I don't want to be responsible!" she said. "What if I succeed? What if, as a result of my intervention, Erin does go to Marion's? What if she only stays there for a few days, and then she bolts?"

"She wouldn't do that," Danielle said.

"She might," Gran said, moving the car half a length forward. "She has a long history of bolting. And if I've made it easy for her to move from the hospital into a situation where Children's Aid have no control over her, then I'll be responsible."

"I don't think they have much control over her now," Sarita said.

"Well, they need to have," Gran said. "She's been seriously injured. She needs proper care, and rest and—"

"But if she goes to a foster home," Danielle said, "she'll definitely bolt from there. So what's the difference?"

"She's more likely to bolt from a foster home than from Marion's," Sarita said. "She loathes foster homes."

"But it's not my responsibility if she leaves her foster home!" Gran said.

We moved forward again. This time we gained a whole car length. The little booth where you pay was just ahead of us. Gran fished her wallet out of her purse.

"Well, I don't know, Gran," I said. "Maybe it's our responsibility to help her go to a place she'll like, where she'll stay. Like Marion's."

"Yes!" Danielle said. "Where she'll be safe and have good food and a place to rest and no guys bugging her and—"

"And time to do her homework," Sarita said.

Gran sighed. "I'll tell you what," she said. "If you girls will do something for me, I'll get in touch with this Ricardo person. I'm not making any promises, but—ah, here we are," she said, coasting up to the booth. She handed over her money, and the car glided out onto the street.

"What do you want us to do?" I said.

"I want you to go over to Marion's after school tomorrow, to help her out. That will free me up to find Ricardo. And I'll need to talk to Erin again, too."

"What do we do when we get there?" Sarita said.

"Marion will tell you," Gran said. "Cleaning, possibly. Or preparing food. Whatever she needs. Your

company will be a real tonic for her. You can tell
her how you wound me around your collective little
finger. She'll get a kick out of that."

"Why do you need to see Erin again?" I said.

"If she'll promise to stay at Marion's," Gran said.
"Even for a couple of weeks, I'll feel much better
about the whole thing."

"What if that guy won't let her go to Marion's?"
Sarita said. "What do we do then?"

"We'll cross that bridge when we come to it,"
Gran said.

At four o'clock the following afternoon, all five of us
piled into Marion's tiny little house. I made a salad
and a macaroni-and-cheese casserole, and while
that was in the oven, I cleaned the bathroom.
Sarita and Wing made a double batch of oatmeal-
chocolate-chip cookies. Danielle dusted, changed
the sheets on Marion's bed, and helped her wash
and dry her hair. And Jean Paul vacuumed the
whole house, top to bottom.

When we were finished, we had tea and cookies
in Marion's front room.

"My goodness," she said. "Such energy. Such
kindness."

"Such cookies," Jean Paul said, passing the
plate to Wing.

Wing took three. "You know that game where

you're supposed to decide what you'd take to a desert island?" he said. "When your ship goes down, or something? Well, most people choose their favorite books or their favorite music, but I could never figure out how you'd keep the books dry, when you were swimming from the sinking ship. Or how you'd get new batteries for your CD player. Anyway, what I'd take is chocolate. Chocolate is the best!"

"Better than girls?" Jean Paul said.

Wing smiled a half smile, tilted his head from one side to the other, and grinned. "Well...," he said, "if girls were an option..."

Jean Paul raised his eyebrows and passed me the plate of cookies. I passed it to Marion.

"Did Gran tell you how we worked her over last night?" I said.

She chortled. "She did, indeed. She sounded rather amused by the whole thing. I do hope she can convince that Children's Aid fellow to let Erin come."

"Maybe we should have a backup plan," I said. "In case she can't."

"I could disguise myself as an orderly," Jean Paul said, "and bring Erin out in a laundry bag."

Danielle shook her head. "Macho man," she said.

Sarita's eyes glowed. "That's actually not a bad idea," she said. "Not the laundry bag part, but we could smuggle her out. Take her some clothes, and — "

"I have some jeans I'm going to give her," I said. "And some runners."

"I have a sweater," Sarita said.

"A coat," I said. "She'll need a coat. Does anybody — "

Marion's cell phone rang. She picked it up, then mouthed the word "Zoe."

"Ah," she said. "He agreed to see you? That's wonderful."

Gran must have asked her about us then. Checking that we'd showed up.

"Yes, they're still here," Marion said. "They've done a week's work in two hours. I don't know how I can possibly repay them. They've been marvelous."

Jean Paul waved his hands around to include all of us. "It's been cool," he said.

The rest of us nodded. It had.

CHAPTER 21

"What about a wheelchair?" Jean Paul said. Erin's hospital bed was propped up higher today. Her bandage was smaller, and her face less swollen. "Sure," she said. "They had me in one this morning. You get them out at the desk."

Jean Paul nodded to Wing and they headed out the door. Two minutes later, they were back—Wing pushing, Jean Paul riding.

Erin pulled my arm and whispered in my ear. "I've got no underwear on," she said. "And my gown's really short."

We sent the guys out of the room. Erin held her gown down and swung her legs over the edge of the bed. We draped a blanket over her shoulders; Danielle took one arm, I took the other, and Sarita held the chair steady. When Erin was settled, we found a second blanket in the closet and tucked it around her.

Jean Paul pushed, and he did it a little fast, I guess, because the rest of us had to run to keep up. Erin loved it, but the hospital people didn't. We got kicked out of the radiology department, the emergency department, the main lobby, the chapel, the gift shop, and the halls of three different wards. The only place we didn't get kicked out of was the cafeteria; but Jean Paul wasn't doing wheelies there, so Erin wasn't squealing. Even so, we came close to getting turfed out of there, too. We were sitting at a big table in the corner, sharing a bag of potato chips. Wing had a sheet of why-did-the-chicken-cross-the-road jokes somebody had e-mailed him, and we were in such a crazy mood, we thought they were hilarious. After the second warning from an exceedingly grim-faced security guard, Danielle snatched Wing's paper, folded it, and tucked it into the big front pocket on her overalls.

Wing had been staring at Erin ever since we got there; he hadn't even tried to hide it. But it was even more obvious once we sat down.

"I know I look like death warmed over," Erin said. "But you don't have to gawk at me like that. You don't have to rub it in."

"I'm not!" he said. "I mean, I..."

Sarita and I looked at each other, then at Erin, then back at each other again, waiting for the explosion. If Wing didn't back off, if he didn't go into an immediate groveling act, Erin's tongue was quite capable of ripping him to shreds. It would slice through him like a hot knife through butter.

Wing is an extremely appealing-looking guy, sort

of innocent and mischievous at the same time.

"Death warmed over is a little extreme," he said. "You look a little rough, maybe. A little ratty around the edges..."

"Thanks a lot," she said.

"Hey, no offense! It's temporary, right? Anyway, if I was gawking, it's because you almost died! If it wasn't for the doctors—"

"And the nurses," Erin added.

"Sure," he said. "The nurses take care of you. Right. But it's the doctors who call the shots. I've been thinking about that ever since we got here. Like how maybe I could do that, study medicine and everything. Then I could save people's lives too. That would be so incredibly cool. All the work, all the years of school, they'd be worth it."

"All the tuition fees, all the student loans," Jean Paul said. "The huge debt you'd have when you're finally finished."

"Yeah!" Wing said. "Even that. Wow! I'm a new man! I can hardly wait to go home and start studying."

Now we all gawked at him.

"Feel free," Jean Paul said. "If you're so pressed for time."

Wing shrugged. "I'll start tomorrow," he said. He looked around the cafeteria. "Just think!" he said. "Maybe someday I'll be wearing a white coat too!"

Danielle turned toward Erin. "Speaking of white coats," she said, "Are the doctors still pushing that foster home thing?"

Erin rolled her eyes. "They sent this delegation of suits up to see me yesterday. You wouldn't believe these people. They're totally rigid, like, totally. I told them I had a place to stay, a really good place, but they wouldn't even listen. According to them, I do it their way or I stay here until I rot. So, of course, I lost it. I said I'd go to a foster home when hell freezes over and the devil learns to skate, which was stupid, because it just made them even madder. They already think I'm the bitch from hell."

"Gran's trying to help," I said. "She was talking to that Ricardo guy about Marion."

"Ricardo has the imagination of a flea," Erin said. "I mean, you'd think somebody whose job was working with kids would have a clue about what makes them tick."

"Gran's kind of formidable," I said. "If anybody can convince him, it would be her."

"Huh," Erin said. "I wish. But I'm not holding my breath. I have this horrible feeling I'm going to have to do it. I'm going to have to go to one of those places, and I'll hate it. I always hate them. There'll be something about it that drives me completely insane, like some creepy guy snooping through my underwear, or a bunch of drippy-nosed brats jumping all over my bed. Or one of these really overbearing motherly types who calls me dear all the time, but who really loathes me. I figure I'll last about a week before I split. A week at the most. And that's scary. I mean, I can't even walk right yet."

"How do you feel about going to Marion's?" Danielle said.

Erin shrugged. "She's not a foster mother. There aren't any guys there," she flashed her eyes at Wing and Jean Paul. "And there aren't any kids. And she needs help, so it wouldn't have the same, you know, feeling about it. She needs me and I need her. I'm not promising I'll stay forever or anything, but..."

"We've been thinking," Sarita said. "Maybe we can get you out of here. If you want us to, that is."

Jean Paul lowered his voice and leaned across the table. "I made this escape plan," he said. He pulled a notebook from his backpack and flipped it open. "If I do say so myself, it's actually quite brilliant."

Danielle reached over as if to snatch it from his hand. "You're taking over, or what?" she said.

"Lay off, Dani, will you?" He looked at Erin. "Can I tell you about it? I mean, if you don't like it or you want to improve it or anything, that's fine with me."

"Sure," Erin said. "Anything that will get me out of here would be great."

Jean Paul glanced at the table of nurses beside us, leaned forward, and whispered, "Maybe we should, like, keep our voices down?"

It was a great plan. The first part was to get the hospital people used to seeing us there, a group of kind-of-noisy kids, one of whom (Sarita) would wear a head scarf that completely covered her hair. The second part was an elaborate identity switch. On the last day, the day we liberated Erin, five visitors would go in and six would leave — the sixth being Erin, now disguised in the head scarf and Sarita's jacket. Sarita would wear the padded vest Jean Paul would smuggle in underneath his coat, the vest that would eventually go to Erin.

There was only one problem.

"What about the hospital?" Sarita said. "One of their patients has just disappeared. They're hardly going to ignore that. And that social worker guy, he's not going to ignore it either. And he's going to know exactly where she is, and—"

"Uh-oh," I said. "Trouble."

Sarita nodded. "We'll probably get charged with kidnapping or something. Your grandmother will get charged with kidnapping. And Marion."

"Shoot!" Erin said. "You're right, you know. I'm a ward of Children's Aid. They own me." She sighed loudly. "And it all sounded like so much fun."

Sarita grinned. "I've got another idea," she said. "You've got two weeks to go, Erin, right?"

Erin nodded. She looked sad.

"If you really work hard at being a pain in the butt," Sarita said, "everybody will be standing there cheering when you leave. They'll probably be pushing you out the door."

Erin roared with laughter. "You mean I should

try to be a pain? I should work at it? Wow!"

Danielle was grinning too. "Exaggerate it," she said. "You can do it, Erin. I know you can."

"Sure," Erin said. She looked at Jean Paul, then at the rest of us. "I'm really grateful for all this," she said. "The visit, the escape plan, everything. You guys caring enough to think it up. It means a lot. I mean, two of you've never even met me before. Well, that's, well...that's really great. It's like, I don't know, Christmas or something."

Danielle rolled her eyes.

Sarita wriggled her fingers in the air. "Ick," she said. "Don't go doing a personality change on us. We won't know who we're dealing with!"

Wing pushed Erin back to her room. When we got there, it was wall-to-wall people, so many that they were spilling out into the passageway between the beds. They were Meiying's family: her grandparents, her parents, her brother, her aunts, her uncles, and her cousins. Wing talked to them in Chinese, then translated. They were having a celebration because they'd just found out that Meiying doesn't have some awful disease; she has something that's hardly awful at all.

As soon as they realized that Erin was Meiying's roommate, everybody moved out into the hall, so we could get Erin through to her bed. Then, everybody moved back in again and started passing food to us—baskets and baskets of it: spring rolls, and shrimp rolls, and sticky rice wrapped in leaves, and dumplings, and something called pot stickers. They had paper plates, too, and napkins; and little containers of dipping sauce, three kinds of it. They even helped Sarita find the vegetarian stuff.

We ate everything, every last delicious little mouthful. Then Wing made a speech, thanking everybody and telling them how glad we were that Meiying was okay. We didn't know what he was saying at the time, of course, only later. Then when we were leaving, all the visitors said, in English, how happy they were to meet us. And we said how happy we were, too. And it was true, we were.

CHAPTER 22

I burst out the main door of the school and there
was Alexei, standing on the sidewalk, looking up
at me and grinning from ear to ear. I smiled
back; I couldn't help myself. Then I saw it wasn't
me he was waiting for. Sherry, his girlfriend, was
right behind me.

I could have avoided them. I could have whipped
back into the school like I'd forgotten something,
but there was a crush of people behind me. Besides,
he'd already seen me. If I took off, he'd think I was
too chicken to meet her.

He introduced us, and we checked each other
out—the friend-who's-a-girl and the girlfriend. She
had clear, fair skin and straight red hair and she
looked great, even up close. I hated to admit it, but
she did.

He put his hand on my shoulder. "So, how old is
Sherry?" he said. "Guess."

Her coat was open, her sweater was tight, and
you could see everything she had, which was plenty.
I shrugged. "Seventeen? Eighteen? I don't know."

Sherry tossed her hair over her shoulder and

laughed. "Fifteen," she said. Then she slid her eyes toward Alexei. "A mature fifteen." She leaned toward Alexei and kissed him on the mouth. It was a lingering kiss, a this-is-MY-boyfriend kiss.

Fine, I thought. Enjoy your mouthful of whiskers. See if I care.

"So," I said, in my best super-cheerful voice. "Are you walking home, Alexei?"

Sherry eyed me suspiciously. "You live near each other?"

"Right next door," I said.

We walked side by side, Alexei in the middle. Sherry slipped her arm around Alexei's waist. I nudged him with my arm. "Written any more poems?" I said.

His eyes darted toward mine. It was not a friendly dart.

Sherry looked blank. "Poems?" she said. "What poems?"

Alexei's arm slid around her shoulders as he guided her around the back end of a car blocking the sidewalk. As I dropped behind them, Sherry hooked her fingers into the back pocket of his jeans. He whispered something into her ear. Her eyes flicked back to me, and she laughed.

The house was empty when I got home. I kicked my runners off, then pitched them, full force, down the hall, all the way to the kitchen.

It was three hours before anybody showed up.

Three hours of stewing; mostly about Alexei and whatever awful comment he had made to Sherry that made her laugh, but also about where Gran was, and what I was supposed to do about supper, because she hadn't left a note. Which was extremely unusual. Gran loves notes; she always leaves them, for everybody, so I was kind of worried. I even phoned Marion a few times, but nobody was there either.

Of course, Mom and Dad were late too. Sitting there, waiting, I kept thinking about the rant I used to get from Dad when I came home late. How he couldn't believe I hadn't phoned. How worried sick he was. He'd throw in my absent sense of responsibility, too, and how self-absorbed I was.

Dad came in first, but Mom was right behind him. I hardly recognized her. She'd had her hair all cut off in one of those really short, guy cuts; and it wasn't brown and curly any more, it was bright yellow and stood up straight, in spikes. And she had two new piercings in one ear.

"What have you done to yourself?" I squealed.

"You don't like it?" she said.

Dad put his arm around her shoulders. "Well, I love it. She looks young. She looks sparkly! Don't you think she looks sparkly, Kat? Don't you think she looks about twenty?"

"When did she have me, then? When she was five?" I sneered.

He chucked me under the chin like I was three years old. "Don't be such a grump," he said. "Well, we're off to play indoor soccer. We just came back for our shoes. Unless," he added, raising his eyebrows and giving Mom this really flirty look out of the corner of his eye, "we decide to skip soccer and go dancing."

He did this goofy little dance step then, like he was some dopey teenager, trying to look cool. I don't know why, but that really pissed me off. Then Mom giggled. That pissed me off even more.

"I don't believe this," I said. "Talk about self-absorbed! Ever since we moved here, you've been like that. I go up to the attic to see you, just to say "hi," and you can hardly drag your eyes away from your computers. We never do anything together anymore. We never talk, you just work, work, work, all the time. Or go out with your friends. Or go dancing. I mean, talk about irresponsible. And insensitive, and uncaring, and shallow and—"

"Now just a minute, young lady," Dad said. "I can see you're upset, but I'm not taking lip like that."

"You're over two hours late and you never even called!" I shouted. "You figured Gran was here, right? Good old Gran, she'll look after everything, right? But guess what? She wasn't here, either! And she still isn't! And she didn't even leave a note. And she's not at Marion's. Nobody is. I phoned about a zillion times. Anything could have happened—a car accident, Marion had a fall, anything."

Mom closed her eyes and shook her head. "Kat," she said. "Simmer down. Are you sure Zoe didn't leave a note? Could you have missed it? She always leaves a note!"

"I'm not a blithering idiot!" I screamed.

Mom ran to the kitchen, presumably to phone Marion. Dad just stood there, looking all confused and wounded and everything. Then he switched into guilt-trip mode. "That was an extremely rude, extremely overblown reaction on your part. You'd think we'd come home dead drunk, not just excited about a cute new look for your mother."

I glared at him through slitted eyes, then followed Mom into the kitchen. She looked deflated, like a balloon gone flat. "They've gone somewhere," she said.

I shrugged. "Maybe."

She sighed. "I'm sorry we didn't call."

"I'm sorry I was so rude," I said. I put my arm around her. "Your hair looks okay, actually. I mean, once I get used to it, I'll probably like it a lot."

She put her arm around me, too. "Why don't we see what we can find for supper."

"I was going to do it," I said, "but there's hardly any food and I couldn't think of what to make."

She poked around in the fridge, then the cupboards. "Soup," she said, "grilled cheese sandwiches, and," she pulled a plastic bag of coleslaw from the crisper, "salad!"

Then Dad came in, all serious and purposeful, but at that very moment Gran came bursting in the back door.

"Sorry, sorry, sorry," she said. "I meant to phone, but I just haven't had a minute." Then she caught sight of Mom. "Oh, my goodness! Don't you look just so spiffy! So young! So vibrant! You look like Kat's sister, not her mother."

"Exactly," I said. I put my arm around Dad's waist and tweaked his paunch.

Gran collapsed into a chair. "Well," she said. "You won't believe this, but I got a call this afternoon, telling me Erin was being discharged from the hospital. Today! To Marion's! So I had to scurry around, let me tell you. First I had to help Marion set up Erin's room, then we got supper under control, and after that, we buzzed over to the hospital to pick up Erin. Well, the poor child, she had hardly a stitch to her name, and no underwear at all, so we did a quick tour of Wal-Mart, and my goodness, I am exhausted! And I never did get to the grocery store. I'm surprised you found anything to eat at all."

"Well, it's not fancy," Mom said. "But there's plenty of it. Why don't you sit down and have some."

"I think I'll just have a cup of tea," Gran said. "I'm too bushed to eat."

"I'll get it, Gran," I said. "How do you think Erin and Marion are going to get along?"

"I have to admit I was a little nervous about leaving them alone together."

"Yeah," I said. "I can believe it." I poured her tea, then cut a sandwich into quarters and put two of them on her saucer. When I passed it to her, my hand sort of brushed her shoulder. It wasn't planned, it just happened.

She patted my hand. I sat down beside her. "Erin's been really nice lately, though," I said.

My personal opinion, which I did not share, was that Erin was being too nice, too sweet. I figured she was faking it so everybody would keep on helping her. Or maybe not. Maybe the old, explosive Erin wasn't the real person, either. Maybe she was just so ticked off with her life, she couldn't help being such a misery. And now that things were looking up, we were seeing the real her.

"She has been nice," Gran said. "She's always been nice with me."

"Not with me," I said.

"So I gather."

I licked a blob of melted cheese from my hand. "I hope she won't, like, blow up, or anything. I'm not trying to turn you against her or anything, Gran. I'm just being honest." Which was true, I was. Erin could get really ugly, really fast, and you didn't necessarily see it coming. What if she mouthed off at Marion and they got in a big fight and everything? What if the whole experiment went down the toilet?

Mom and Dad had only seen Erin's sweet side

too. "I think," Dad said, "that we have to give Erin the opportunity to be the nice person she can be. We shouldn't assume that the more dysfunctional stuff is the real her, any more than being nice all the time is the real her." He reached his hand across the table to touch mine. "We all mess up sometimes," he said. "Even me."

"And me," Mom said. She looked sad. And really pretty.

"And me," I said. "You look great, Mom," I added. "It was just kind of a shock." I lifted my hair off my neck. "Maybe I should have a makeover too. What do you think about purple spikes and a tongue piercing? And, I don't know, should I do my navel, while I'm at it?"

They all stared at me. "Just kidding," I said. "For now, anyway."

"Whew," Dad said. "One groovy chick is all I can handle. Say," he added, sitting bolt upright in his chair, "I just had an idea. Let's have a party. To celebrate Erin's recovery."

Gran beamed. "What a wonderful idea!"

"A sleepover!" I said. "You guys could move down to my room and we could have it in the attic." I leapt to my feet and paced up and down the kitchen. "Two on your bed, one on the couch, and one on the floor. Great! Can we do it this weekend?"

"Just hold on a minute," Dad said. "You're away ahead of me. I was thinking of a party for every-

body. Zoe, Marion, your friends, their parents...
What do you think, Zoe? It's your house, after all."

"I like the idea of having adults too," Gran said.

I sat down again, hard. "You'd invite everybody's
parents? You don't even know them! You've never
even met!"

"Exactly," Mom said. "They're new, we're new,
our kids are friends. Why not?"

"You can't invite people you don't know!" I said.
"What will you talk about?"

Dad laughed. "Our kids, for starters."

I folded my arms. "I don't know about this," I
said. "What if they don't come?"

"Then they don't," Mom said, shrugging. "But I
think they will. We'll make it a dinner, a potluck.
People are comfortable with that. We wouldn't turn
down an invitation to meet your friends' parents.
What makes you think they'd be any different?"

Gran looked at her watch, then pushed herself
away from the table. "News time," she said. "Who
wants to watch?"

"I'll clean up," I said. Dad went with Gran into
the front room to watch TV. Mom stayed to help.

I carried the dirty dishes over to the counter. "I
heard from Suze yesterday," I said.

Mom was rinsing plates in the sink, then stacking
them in the dishwasher. "And how's Suze?" she said.

I pulled the letter from my pocket and handed it
to her.

Chapter Twenty-Two

Dear Kat,
Sorry about not writing. I was going out with
Kenny again, and I didn't want you to know.
Anyhow, I finally clued in to what a total
turnip he is, and broke up with him.
What really blows me away is that Mom
broke up with Sleazy Arthur the same day!
She says he was a T.I.H. boyfriend.
Temporary Insanity of the Hormones.
And guess what? Pen's dog, a golden retriev-
er, had a bout of T.I.H. with a big black Lab
who showed up about five minutes after
Pen's dog went into heat, and when the pups
are old enough, we're getting one! I absolutely
cannot wait! AND Mom and I are going to
Florida for spring break, just the two of us.

Love ya,
Suze.

P.S. Pen has loosened up a lot. She thinks
I'm a riot.

Mom grinned when she handed the letter back.
"Good for Suze," she said. "She sounds great."

CHAPTER 23

Including Mom and Dad and Gran and me, there were fifteen people for dinner: six kids and nine adults.

Sarita's family are vegetarians, so Gran and I made a huge meatless lasagna and a humongous salad. The Shahs brought samosas; the Vincents, a spicy bean-and-rice casserole. Wing and his dad lugged in enough spring rolls to feed an army, and a tub of sauce to go with them. Erin and Marion made a three-layer double-chocolate cake, and Mom and Dad contributed the wine. That was for the adults, of course. The kids got the smallest possible amount, like about one half of one swallow, and we only got that because Gran wanted to propose a toast.

She held her glass high in the air. "To Erin," she said. "To her continued good health, and to her happiness in her new home."

Then we had to raise our glasses in the air too, and clink them against everybody else's glass and say "to Erin" with every clink. After that we got our pathetic little drink.

Erin was so overwhelmed, she was almost bawling, but Gran and Marion gave her hugs, and then I gave her one, and Danielle and Sarita put their arms around both of us. Jean Paul was looking like he was just itching to get in on it too; but Danielle kicked him, so he and Wing made a chair out of their hands and paraded Erin up and down the hall, until she begged for mercy.

The food was laid out on the kitchen counter and table, so everybody filled a plate out there, then moved into the dining room or the front room to sit down. The way it turned out, the kids all sat at Marion's patio table in the front room, and the adults gathered at the dining room table. But Gran opened the big, heavy sliding door between the rooms, so we were hardly separated at all.

I was terrified there'd be long silences when nobody knew what to say, but it wasn't like that at all. After everybody complimented everybody else's food, the adults started talking about where they'd moved from and why they'd come; and the kids, about how awful it was that the adults all knew each other now, and how we'd never be able to get away with anything. But the most interesting conversation involved Erin, about her having been in a coma. Everybody wanted to know what it was like: if she could hear or feel things, or if she could remember anything about it.

"It's just a big blank," she said. "One minute

there was this freaked-out guy swinging a big black frying pan at my head, then the next thing I knew, I was waking up in the hospital."

Of course, all the adults were adopting Erin, which was a bit much, but in a way, it was good she was getting all that attention, because it sort of made up for how miserable Sarita and I had been. And Danielle too, though she wasn't nearly as bad as we were. Erin didn't carry a grudge though, you had to say that for her. She was really nice to everybody, the whole time. She didn't blow up even once.

Later, after the dishes had been cleared away, Marion organized some card games. She wanted us kids to play too, but we slipped up to the attic, listened to music, and talked.

We had questions for Erin, too: stuff Sarita and Danielle and I had always wondered about, but had been kind of afraid to ask. But Jean Paul didn't mind asking anybody anything.

"If I'm being too curious, Erin," he said, "all you have to do is say so." He looked across at Danielle and grinned. "I've been told to shut up so many times, I almost think it's my name."

Erin was sitting beside me on the floor, leaning back against Mom and Dad's bed. She didn't mind the questions at all; I think she actually liked them.

And this time, she told the truth. I knew, because Ricardo told Marion, who told Gran, who told me. I didn't tell anyone else though. I let Erin do that.

The truth was worse than any of those stories she'd made up, and sadder: a father she'd never known, an alcoholic mother, and one foster home after another, starting when she was only six.

"Part of all that bouncing from one foster home to another was my fault," Erin said. "I can see that now. You wouldn't believe how awful I was — temper tantrums, screaming fits, the works. I mean, it's no wonder nobody wanted to keep me very long. And I was always getting into fights with the other foster kids. Once, I even got my arm broken. Then, when I was fourteen, I started running away. I'd live in the street for a couple of days, then I'd go back to the foster home, then I'd get fed up and leave again. After a while, I stopped going back.

"I thought I was cool," she said. "And free. Ricardo used to plead with me to smarten up and get back to school and everything, but I wouldn't listen. Not for a long time."

Sarita, sprawled on the couch on her stomach, had one arm draped over the side. "Were you a real street kid?" she said. "Did you sleep outside and everything?"

Erin shrugged. "In the summer, sometimes, but not when it was cold. We stayed in squats, mostly — abandoned buildings with no water and no heat. Then, this girl I knew froze to death. Well, that's what we thought at the time, but somebody else said she had tuberculosis, so maybe she died from that.

"Anyway, that kind of woke me up. So I talked the manager of this creepy restaurant into letting me stay there at night, in return for cleaning, but there were other people there too. They were so awful, I was afraid to turn my back on them. Like that guy who stole all my stuff—he was selling it to buy dope! When he finally admitted it, I went ballistic." She touched her head near the front, the part that was shaved, probing it gently with her fingers. "And you know what happened then."

Danielle was perched on the arm of the couch closest to Sarita's feet. "That's so sad," she said. "Your whole life's been sad. But you're so strong, the way you went back to school and everything."

"That's for sure," Jean Paul said. "Are you going to be okay at Marion's? There's not too much work or anything, is there? I could help, if there is."

Erin shook her head. "She's great," she said. "I feel like I've died and gone to heaven." She slid her eyes toward mine and smiled. "The other person who's been great is Zoe."

I nodded. "You're sort of like her, you know?" I said. "You both say what you think."

Erin laughed. "You mean, we shoot our mouths off?"

"Well..." I said.

Wing put one of his CDs on then, one with a great beat. Then he and Jean Paul started twirling themselves around on Mom and Dad's swivel chairs, seeing who could go the longest without falling off. Wing lost.

When Dad called me downstairs, I was halfway there already, heading to the kitchen for pop.

"Alexei's here," Dad said. "I tried to get him to come in, but he'd rather not."

He was standing in the vestibule, leaning against the wall. He tilted his head toward the front room. "You are having a party?" he said.

"Sort of. You want to come in? My friends are upstairs."

He shook his head. "I came to say good-bye," he said.

I swung the door partly shut behind me. "Where are you going?"

He grinned. "Timmins. To be a car mechanic, like Yuri. Auntie Tatyana owns a service station."

"But what about your...school?" I said. What I almost said was, "What about your girlfriend?"

He shrugged. "I will go to night school, like Yuri. I will save much money for university. This is good, yes?"

"You're going right now? Right this very minute?"

He looked at his watch, and shrugged.

"Alexei, this is awful! You can't just—"

He nodded solemnly. "It is necessary," he said. He gave the hall door a little extra push, slid his arm around my shoulders and buried his face in my neck. "Come outside with me," he murmured. "We should say good-bye properly."

My brain knew I should push him away, fast,

but he raised his head, then, and looked deep into
my eyes. I looked deep into his. My knees felt weak.
Then the hall door opened behind me.

"Oops!" Erin said. "I thought somebody was leaving. I was just going to say thanks and—I mean, I
was just coming to look for Kat, and..."

Alexei smoothed my hair back from my forehead, kissed me on the cheek, then slid out the
door. I just stood there, stunned.

"I didn't know," Erin said. "I'm really sorry, Kat."

"He's moving!" I said. "Up north, somewhere."

"He's important?" she asked.

I sighed. "He was."

Erin was really nice. She just stood there quietly,
letting me be.

"I just don't get it, Erin," I said. "I was crazy about
him, but—"

"He wasn't good for you?"

I nodded.

"You can know a guy's no good for you, but
want him just the same," she said.

My eyes filled with tears. Erin grabbed the sleeve
of her sweater—a yellow cotton one, formerly Jean
Paul's—and blotted my face with it quite firmly.

"It's one of life's mysteries," she said. "I've seen
it before. I've even been there." She looked at me
shrewdly. "You didn't do anything stupid, did you?"

I shook my head. When I looked at her then, I
felt like I was seeing her for the first time. Truly

seeing her, and liking what I saw. "I'll tell you about it sometime," I said. "Thanks. Thanks a lot."

She shrugged. "Any time. Hey, we were thinking about going out back, to play hockey."

"But what about nets and sticks and stuff?"

"The guys brought everything with them," she said. "Come on. They're bouncing off the walls up there. They'll be wrestling on the floor next."

The lane was icy, with a scattering of snow. There were two streetlights. We set the net between them, then divided ourselves into teams. I was with Wing and Danielle.

Nobody had skates, but we had five regular hockey sticks, a goalie stick, a puck, and one helmet. Erin pulled it carefully over her head, snapped the chin strap and swung the wire-mesh mask over her face.

"Cool!" she said. "I may wear this for the rest of my life!" She took a practice run down the lane, maneuvering her stick from side to side, guiding an imaginary puck in front of her. When she turned back to face us, she looked strong, like her old self again. "Okay!" she yelled. "Go for it!"

I'm not all that great at games, especially the kind that involve small, hard objects whizzing through the air. Every muscle in my body wants to get me out of there fast. But when the puck skittered to my feet, I gritted my teeth, and flicked it neatly away from the net.

Danielle was a fantastic goalie. Nothing got by her, even when she moved out of the net. Erin, of course, was relentless. She chopped away with her stick, fighting for the puck every chance she got. But it was Sarita who surprised me the most. I was counting on her being a wimp too, but she wasn't. She shot the puck hard and straight and she used her elbows as weapons, and they were wickedly effective. I watched her closely. I watched all of them closely. Then I started playing like they did. Instead of standing back, waiting for the puck to land at my feet, I raced toward it and whacked it as hard as I could.

The streetlights made patterns and shadows on the snow, and when we laughed and called out to each other, we could see our breath. The only problem was we couldn't always see the puck. Once, Jean Paul and I went roaring down the lane after it, then collapsed, giggling, into a snowbank when we couldn't find it.

There was only one tense moment: when Erin fell. We all raced toward her, terrified she'd hurt her head, even with the helmet on; but she raised herself up on her elbow and laughed, and we all let our breath out. You could actually hear it, this big whooshing sound, the breath-letting-out sound of five people. That made Erin laugh even more.

The best part came right at the end, after Dad called out the door to tell us the party was almost over. The other fathers came out too, right out into the lane, supposedly to help collect the equipment, but really to take a few shots on goal themselves. Then everybody started saying good-bye, and hugging everybody else, because we'd had such a great time.

I didn't notice I'd missed Jean Paul in the hug exchange until Danielle was dragging him away and he started making this little moaning noise in the back of his throat. It was the kind of sound you make when you get your results back from a test, and you see the stupid mistake you made, the one that cost you ten marks.

"What a bozo," he said. "I should have hugged Kat first."

CHAPTER 24

I missed Alexei, but I didn't miss him half as much as everybody thought I did. I wasn't dying, or anything.

Gran thought I was. She thought I was being brave, and hiding it.

"You'll get over him," she said. "He isn't the only wickedly flirtatious heartthrob in the universe."

Mom and Dad weren't exactly oozing sympathy either. I'm sure they were glad he was gone, so they didn't have to worry about me anymore.

Sarita and Danielle were glad he was gone too, only they came right out and said so. They also said he was a mistake, whatever that means. How can a person be a mistake? How can it be a mistake to like somebody?

Then, about two weeks after Alexei left, Gran and I went over to Marion's for dinner. After, when Erin and I went up to her room, the whole miserable story came pouring out—every sordid little detail. How Alexei came on to me, how mean he was, how we sort of made up and I thought he liked me again, the new girlfriend, everything.

"I'd be royally bummed out too," Erin said. "But think how bad you'd feel if you'd done what he wanted. He still would have gone."

I just stared at her. I'd never thought about that before, but it was true. There was no way he would have stayed, not just for me.

That's when I started to take my brain seriously, to make it work for me. So now, when I think about Alexei, I see this eighteen-year-old guy who was really experienced with girls, and who knew exactly what he wanted from them. And then beside him, I see me. Feeling flattered that he liked me, getting blown away by all that sexy romantic stuff. Thinking I was taking care of him—being the soft, tender person he needed right then, helping him with his poetry, comforting him about his family. Only Alexei wasn't taking care of me. He was pushing me in ways I didn't want to be pushed, and he wasn't being nice about it, either.

The thing is, you never really know what a guy is like—whether or not you can trust him, whether or not he really cares about you—until you say "no" when he's bursting for you to say "yes." That's when you find out what he's made of.

I guess what I'm saying is: I could have gotten really messed up over Alexei, but I didn't. I'm proud of that. I handled it okay.

Erin is doing okay too. She and Marion are really funny together. When we were at Marion's that time, and Gran asked them how they were getting along together, they went into this little complaining act.

Erin put on this sly grin. Then she tilted her head toward Marion. "She gets ticked off at me."

Marion snorted. "I do, indeed. She's a bit too casual about the rules for my taste. She can't tell the time, either."

"I'm a teenager!" Erin said. "I go out. Sometimes I forget to tell you."

"Forget, shmorget!" Marion said, laughing. "She's making a point."

Erin raised her eyebrows, all innocence. "Which is?"

"Independence," Marion said. "Pushing the limits. She pretty well does what she wants, but we're adjusting to each other. When she is here, she's superb. She couldn't be better."

Erin popped up and did this little curtsy thing at Marion; then she did it to everybody else. When she sat down, she was grinning all over her face.

After coming home from the hospital, Erin transferred to a new school, one closer to Marion's, and she's made a bunch of new friends. "My guardian angels," she calls them. She never says what they're guarding her from, but whatever it is, it's working.

Since she changed schools, we don't see each other all that often, but we talk on the phone a lot, which seems to work for us. Because however much I like Erin sometimes, we still have a long way to go.

Sarita and Danielle and I are pretty close though. We have lunch together whenever we can, and we study together sometimes, too. Or we go downtown. Sarita knows where to buy stuff cheap.

And then there's Jean Paul.

I used to think he was pretty immature. Now I think that in some ways, he's a sweet, innocent guy who's just learning about girls. But in other ways, he's extremely mature, and extremely understanding. When he comes to my locker, which he does at least three times a day, I can't believe how sweet he is. The other thing I can't believe is how everybody else—all the crowds in the hall and everything—just fades into the background. It's like we're on an island somewhere, just the two of us; and the sun is shining, and the water is lapping against the rocks, and we're staring into each other's eyes, and smiling.

Actually, I think I'm getting just the teeniest bit obsessed with him. I'll be walking home from school, or sitting in class, or in bed trying to go to sleep, and practically all I can think about is how it would be if he was my boyfriend. How I wouldn't have to fight him off all the time, and when we kissed I could let the tingly feelings come, and the shivers, and everything, because I could relax with him. I'd feel safe.

I'm pretty sure about that. I can't believe he's the kind of guy who'd do a number on me to get me to say "yes." If something does start up between us,

I have a very strong feeling that Jean Paul will let me set the pace.

One day, soon, I'm going to check that out.